Magic was one thing.
Miracles were quite another.

Merry felt her first shiver of doubt. Rick was wounded, and he didn't like romance. But there was something about him that made her *want* to see love transform his life.

And then, suddenly, he went very still beside her. Intrigued, she followed his gaze. He stared with his eyes narrowed to a hard squint at Cynthia Forsythe.

Merry started at his deep growl. Every hair on the back of her neck rose up. "You know Cynthia?" she asked.

Something in his face closed and became colder than ice. "I did," he said. "A long time ago."

"I'd be happy to reintroduce you!"

The look he gave her could have stripped paint. "No," he said. "In fact, I'd thank you not to mention me to her."

Merry's heart pounded hard. What could be more perfect? Her last couple—a love-gone-wrong-and-now-made-right story! But a glance into the cast stone of his face made her wonder if even magic could change what she saw there.

Dear Reader,

Let this month's collection of Silhouette Romance books sweep you into the poetry of love!

Roses are red,
or white in the case of these *Nighttime Sweethearts* (SR #1754) by Cara Colter. Scarred both physically and emotionally, this cynical architect will only woo his long-lost love under the protection of night. Can a bright beauty tame this dark beast? Find out in the fourth title of Silhouette Romance's exquisite IN A FAIRY TALE WORLD… miniseries.

Violets are blue,
like the eyes of the ladies' man in Myrna Mackenzie's latest, *Instant Marriage, Just Add Groom* (SR #1755). All business, even in his relationships, this hardened hero would never father a child without the protection of marriage—but he didn't count on falling for the prim bookseller next door!

Cupid's at play,
and he's got the use of more than arrows for matchmaking! Even a blinding blizzard can bring two reluctant people together. Watch the steam rise when a gruff, reclusive writer is stranded with a single mom and her adorable baby in *Daddy, He Wrote* (SR #1756) by Jill Limber.

And magic, too!
With only six days left to break her curse, Cat knew she couldn't count on finding true love. Until she happened upon a dark, reticent veterinarian with a penchant for rescuing animals—and damsels—in distress! You're sure to be enchanted by Shirley Jump's SOULMATES story, *Kissed by Cat* (SR #1757).

May love find *you* this Valentine's Day!
Mavis C. Allen
Associate Senior Editor

Please address questions and book requests to:
Silhouette Reader Service
U.S.: 3010 Walden Ave., P.O. Box 1325, Buffalo, NY 14269
Canadian: P.O. Box 609, Fort Erie, Ont. L2A 5X3

Nighttime
Sweethearts
Cara Colter

SILHOUETTE *Romance*®

Published by Silhouette Books

America's Publisher of Contemporary Romance

Special thanks and acknowledgment are given
to Cara Colter for her contribution to the
IN A FAIRY TALE WORLD… series.

To Judy and Charles Moon
in gratitude for all you do

 SILHOUETTE BOOKS

ISBN 0-373-19754-3

NIGHTTIME SWEETHEARTS

Visit Silhouette Books at www.eHarlequin.com

Printed in U.S.A.

Books by Cara Colter

Silhouette Romance

Dare To Dream #491
Baby in Blue #1161
Husband in Red #1243
The Cowboy, the Baby
  and the Bride-to-Be #1319
Truly Daddy #1363
A Bride Worth Waiting For #1388
Weddings Do Come True #1406
A Babe in the Woods #1424
A Royal Marriage #1440
First Time, Forever #1464
*Husband by Inheritance #1532
*The Heiress Takes a Husband #1538
*Wed by a Will #1544
What Child Is This? #1585
Her Royal Husband #1600
9 Out of 10 Women Can't Be Wrong #1615
Guess Who's Coming for Christmas? #1632
What a Woman Should Know #1685
Major Daddy #1710
Her Second-Chance Man #1726
Nighttime Sweethearts #1754

Silhouette Books

The Coltons
A Hasty Wedding

*The Wedding Legacy

CARA COLTER

shares ten acres in the wild Kootenay region of British Columbia with the man of her dreams, three children, two horses, a cat with no tail and a golden retriever who answers best to "bad dog." She loves reading, writing and the woods in winter (no bears). She says life's delights include an automatic garage door opener and the skylight over the bed that allows her to see the stars at night.

She also says, "I have not lived a neat and tidy life, and used to envy those who did. Now I see my struggles as having given me a deep appreciation of life, and of love, that I hope I succeed in passing on through the stories that I tell."

The Tale of the Bear Who Married a Woman

[Source: Franz Boas, *Tsimshian Mythology*
(Washington, D.C.: United States Government Printing Office, 1916.)]

Once upon a time there lived a widow with a beautiful daughter. Many men asked for the daughter's hand, but the widow declined them all. The mother wanted a son-in-law who had the hands to build a solid canoe. So her advice to her daughter was to feel her suitors' palms. "If they are soft, decline him. If they are rough, accept him."

Her daughter obeyed and refused to be wooed by any of the young men. Until one night, a man came to her bed. She tucked her hands in his and found his palms to be very rough, so she accepted his proposal. Early the next morning, however, he had disappeared. She had never even seen his face. But in front of the house was a tasty fish, left for the girl and her mother.

The girl, her mother and the young man who visited only at night lived this way for some time. The young woman never saw her husband, but every morning she found an animal at the door, each one larger than the last. Because of the animals, the widow became quite rich.

But the widow was eager to see her son-in-law, so one day she waited until he arrived. What she saw was a red bear emerging from the water. He carried two whales, but as soon as he noticed the widow looking at him, he was transformed into a rock, which may be seen up to this day.

Prologue

"Ms. Montrose?" Her secretary paged Merry over the office speakerphone. "Rick Barnett is here to see you."

"Who?" Merry asked, not even trying to keep the edge out of her voice. She did not have time for anyone right now.

"He's the architect. The one you've chosen to build the chapel?"

Oh, yes, the architect. The chapel was the brilliant idea Merry had conceived. Given the amount of romance blossoming at La Torchere resort, where she was a manager, they should have an on-site chapel. People could plan to have weddings here. The resort's owner had been thrilled with her idea, naturally, and had given her the go-ahead via correspondence to look after all the details.

At the time, Merry had been quite pleased with the success of her idea. Now it seemed like small potatoes, compared to what was going on in her *real* life.

She had to play matchmaker for only one more couple,

and the spell that had been placed on her almost seven years ago by her well-meaning—but nonetheless wicked—godmother, Lissa, would be broken!

Broken, broken, broken. She would go from being this wrinkled, bony, gray-haired old crone back to her gorgeous, young self. Closing her eyes, she remembered what she had once looked like: the flawless skin, the waves of auburn hair, the beautiful figure she had taken so for granted.

Yes, Merry Montrose, aka Princess Meredith Montrosa Bessart, was one match away from being restored to her former fabulous life. Not that managing this very exclusive island resort off the coast of Florida didn't have moments so rewarding they took her by surprise, but, really—life as a resort manager or life as a princess? The choice was a no-brainer!

She indulged in a moment's daydreaming. She would be welcomed back to the kingdom of Silestia. There would be parties and celebrations in the streets. She would once again have her life of luxury. She would marry the prince she had been promised to at birth, and their union would provide fabulous business opportunities and contracts. There would be glory and glamour, as was befitting a princess.

But enough daydreaming! The curse had required she match twenty-one couples before her thirtieth birthday. Couple number twenty—that delightful sheik and the lovely Selina Carrington had fallen head over heels for each other—just as Merry had planned. Couple nineteen, Brad Smith and Parris Hammond, were marrying right here at the resort next week.

Time was of the essence now. Only weeks to go before Merry turned thirty. Only one couple left!

Now was not the time for dilly-dallying, but Merry

found herself wasting precious moments fretting over who to match. If it was going to be her last effort, she wanted it to be absolutely perfect. Stacks of papers and files and photographs littered her desk as she debated whose lives to meddle in.

"In the loveliest way, of course," she muttered, holding up a photo of a stunning actress, a regular at La Torchere. "Well beyond her prime," Merry noted, though not unkindly. She shuffled her photos like cards in a deck and came to La Torchere's gardener, also beyond his prime. Was it possible?

"Ms. Montrose?" the secretary's voice came again, uncertainly, over the speakerphone, "Should I send him in?"

"Oh, if you must," Merry said crabbily and slammed the intercom button with the palm of her hand. She put the actress and gardener aside and picked up a photo of an award-winning nuclear physicist and a belly-button-flaunting rock diva. "Too big a stretch," she decided unhappily.

There was that new handyman on the place. Gorgeous. Blond, blue-eyed, the build of a Greek god…

A shadow fell over her, and she looked up. The photos fell from her fingers. "You must be Rick Barnett," she said, her annoyance at this disturbance forgotten.

It's him, she decided, feeling a smile starting inside. So, fate had opted to help her with her final match. It had given her the man, now all she had to do was find the woman. She got up and took his hand, felt the strength in it and the crackle of his fate joining hers.

Merry studied the young man in front of her with avid interest now. The pure power of his build was enough to take a girl's breath away. He was massive at the shoulders, narrow at waist and hips and—she snuck a look as he turned to find his chair—his butt was spectacular.

Once, she could tell, he had been an extremely handsome man. Dark thick hair fell over his brow. His features—forehead, chin, nose, jaw—were chiseled perfection. But now a black patch roguishly covered his left eye and a network of scars, puckered and purplish, ran down the left side of his face. His face was a study in contrasts, one half perfect, the other imperfect, as if the man himself was split in two, light and dark.

"Construction accident," he said, before she could ask.

His voice was like gravel, flat and harsh, a voice that invited no intrusion into his private world and wanted no sympathy. Nonetheless, Merry heard and, glancing up, saw in the dark, ocean blue of the right eye that glared at her— Rick Barnett was a man in pain.

It startled Merry how completely she understood his situation. Had she not been transformed herself? From a woman so beautiful she put the stars to shame, to this? A bony, homely, horrible old crone?

The difference was that she had a chance to break the curse that had been put on her. The man who sat before her was transformed for life, and he looked to be in his mid to late twenties.

The young female rock star? she asked herself, surreptitiously moving the photo back into her range of vision.

No. It would take the most special of women to see beyond surface appearances. Not the rock star, she decided, shuffling that photo to the bottom of the stack.

She studied him carefully and was able to see what had not been taken from him, but what had been given to him. Oh, yes, his looks had been shattered, but she had the sudden sensation of seeing his heart.

Formidable strength, enormous pain and, under it all, an amazing capacity for love.

Love.

It was all she could do not to burst into song. She realized she must be smiling at him with far too much enthusiasm, because he looked at her suspiciously and then got up from his chair and wandered restlessly over to the window.

Merry watched how he moved, fluid, an athlete, and felt a sigh inside of her. She got up and joined him at the window.

"There are a number of possible sites," she said. "That's one over there, by the pool. We want the chapel to be a small, very tasteful building. La Torchere seems to inspire romance." *Especially recently.*

He grunted at that, letting her know exactly what he thought of romance.

"The new owner has agreed with me that offering an entire wedding facility here would be an aesthetic plus for the resort."

"Not to mention financially lucrative?" he asked.

Cynical, Merry thought, and felt her first shiver of doubt. The man was wounded, and he didn't like romance. Magic was one thing. Miracles were quite another.

"I'm interested," she said carefully, "in why you would agree to do a job like this? Something so small? Your reputation, naturally, made me think you would refuse so humble a job."

He was studying the possible building site she had pointed out. If she had hoped his answer would reveal something she could use to find him a match, she was disappointed.

"I needed a break from the pressure of big jobs," he told her.

"Oh," she said, her mind whirling. Maybe he wasn't the one. Maybe she had just leapt to that conclusion. Maybe the actress and the new handyman. She felt a certain reluctance to match up the new handyman.

What was that about?

But before she could consider it further Rick Barnett turned from the window. The hard light in his eye softened. "I felt oddly compelled to be here."

Merry tried not to gasp out loud. Oh! Then it was him! But who would she pair him with? She wanted to hustle him out of her office without ceremony so she could go through her files. She felt a most delicious sense of warmth beginning in her belly.

And she realized, amazed at herself, that it was not completely because she was so close to breaking the curse.

No, there was something about this man, that made her *want* to see love transform his life. Suddenly, he went very still beside her, as if he had stopped breathing.

Intrigued, she went to his side and followed his gaze. He was staring, his eye narrowed to a hard squint, at Cynthia Forsythe, one of the guests whose files Merry had pored over earlier. She would be an ideal candidate for a match—she was young and beautiful and personable.

Except her mother, the famous historical writer, Emma Bluebell Forsythe, had cornered the matchmaking market for her daughter. The woman was intent on finding the perfect mate for Cynthia…and she was utterly insensitive to the fact that her daughter was not interested.

"Cynthia," he said.

Merry started at the deep growl that came from the man beside her. Every hair on the back of her neck rose up.

"You know her?" she asked.

Something in his face closed and became colder than ice. "I did," he said, "a long time ago."

"I'd be happy to reintroduce you!"

The look he gave her could have stripped paint. "No," he said. "In fact, I'd thank you not to mention me to her."

Merry's heart was pounding hard. What could be more perfect? Her last couple—a love-gone-wrong-made-right story!

But a glance into the cast stone of his face made her wonder if even magic could change what she saw there.

Still, she had a soft spot for him, the man who, like her, had been transformed, but unlike her was not ever going back to what he used to be.

How strong was her magic? Dare she waste it on this couple who were far from a sure thing when her whole life was at stake?

She sighed. Oh, how she had cursed this spell that had been put on her. How she had railed against it and wallowed in self-pity over it.

But, ever so reluctantly, Princess Meredith Montrosa Bessart, aka Merry Montrose, realized a truth. She had become a better person than she had been before.

Because, for just the briefest moment in time, just long enough to make up her mind, she was able to put the future happiness of two other people ahead of her own.

Rick and Cynthia it is, Merry decided, and began humming the wedding march. Naturally, he thought she was inspired by the imminent arrival of the new chapel, designed by him, but he winced nonetheless.

Chapter One

"No."

Cynthia Forsythe marveled at the enormous power of that small word. She said it to her mother, the famous writer Emma Bluebell Forsythe, rarely, and she expected to feel guilty, saying it now.

Instead, she felt a delicious and rather wicked sense of delight.

Her mother, dressed in a Chanel gown with her hair dyed a new shade of dark brown, stood in the door between their adjoining suites.

"No?" her mother repeated, as if she might not have heard correctly. "Cynthia, of course you are coming. I've met a real live baron. From Germany. He's only a year or two older than you and he is one of the world's wealthiest industrialists! Isn't that exciting?"

"No," Cynthia repeated.

"It's not exciting?" her mother said, her hazel eyes wide with bafflement.

Cynthia really didn't think it was that exciting—no more exciting than the newspaper magnate, the oil tycoon or the banker, but she clarified. "No, I'm not coming out tonight."

"Dinner is going to be exquisite, and I understand there is a show after that we really can't miss. Oh, how I love it here at La Torchere, Cynthia. It's better than Tuscany, which I must admit was a bit of a disappointment. But this place is so exclusive and classy, and there are just oodles of well-heeled people here. You can't miss it. You simply have to come!"

Cynthia was a trifle amazed to find she didn't have to, and she wasn't going to. She folded her arms over her chest and said that powerful little word again.

Her mother's eyes filmed over with tears, but she was quick enough with her handkerchief that her makeup was not affected by the little cloudburst. "Why are you being like this?"

"Mother, I'm just tired."

"That's why this holiday is for you! I've worked you much too hard. I should have broken the Civil War into chunks, instead of tackling the whole thing at once. Now you're exhausted, and unhappy, and it's my fault. I am honor-bound to fix it."

"No," Cynthia repeated again. That heady word was proving absolutely addictive. It was true she did work hard. Her mother was known to the world as Emma Bluebell Forsythe, writer of historical volumes of nonfiction that consistently made the bestseller lists.

The research for each novel was meticulous, and Cynthia's job also involved keeping her mother's many social activities and obligations sorted out and scheduled.

It was true that as her mother's personal assistant Cynthia was exhausted.

Unhappy? She supposed there was truth in that, too,

though she didn't feel particularly unhappy. She wasn't sure when she'd last felt anything at all. She was going through her life like a wooden puppet, making the motions, dancing the dance, but strangely detached from the whole process.

"Mother, if this holiday is truly for me, could you just let me have some breathing space, some time to myself?"

"Well, of course, it's truly for you," her mother wailed, "but I'm the one who knows what is best for you!"

Cynthia closed her eyes. And tonight that was a wealthy German industrialist. Last night it had been the exceedingly boring, but rich, Maxwell Davies. Tomorrow, unless she put her foot down, it would be Count Dracula if he was on vacation here and single.

There was a loud knock on her mother's door, and then a deep, masculine voice called, "Bluebird, what on earth is the hold up?"

Cynthia opened her eyes to see Jerome Carrington coming though the door of her mother's suite.

Jerome was a silver-haired dynamo whom her mother had recently met. He was the only one who could get away with calling Emma Forsythe Bluebird. The occasional very good, very old friend was allowed Bluebell, but no derivatives of the unusual name had ever been allowed.

"Good evening, Cynthia," he said, and then turned to her mother with a stern expression on his handsome face. "You said that you would be outside my room at nine o'clock precisely, and here it is, nearly nine-fifteen."

Her mother glared at Jerome. Not only was he the only one who called her Bluebird, he was certainly the only one who would have the nerve to reprimand her over such a small thing as fifteen minutes of tardiness.

Emma was a shrewd judge of character, though, and had

obviously decided Jerome was not one to accept any form of excuse. Naturally, she blamed Cynthia for her lateness.

"It's Cynthia's fault," she wailed prettily. "I've been standing here *forever* trying to talk sense into her. I have the most wonderful evening lined up for all of us, and she says she's not coming. Jerome, talk to her!"

"All right," he said, and he turned to Cynthia. She saw the loveliest spark of mischief in those steel gray eyes. "My dear," he said to her. "How old are you?"

"Twenty-six," she replied.

"Hmm. Plenty old enough to be making your own plans for the evening. Bluebird?" And he crooked his elbow to Emma.

Emma sputtered and looked between him and her daughter and back to him. He did not remove his arm, but arched a questioning eyebrow at her.

"Oh," she sputtered, "all right then. Cynthia, you and I will talk later."

Much later, Cynthia hoped as she shut the door of her private suite on the departing couple. She looked around. She loved her rooms. They consisted of a small living area, an island kitchen, and a small alcove for dining. There was one bedroom and a bathroom. Outside, a patio with deep inviting deck furniture stretched the full length of the ground-floor suite, and both the bedroom and living room had French doors that opened onto that outdoor living area. It was separated from the public walkways by a bevy of gorgeous flowering shrubs and gardens. Beyond those gardens and pathways, in the distance, Cynthia could glimpse the endless blue of the sea.

The color scheme was serene and tropical. The furniture was not just beautiful, but also comfy and inviting. Everything at La Torchere Resort was a delight to the senses, including these lovely rooms that seemed to be awash in light and cheeriness.

Her own apartment at home did not give her this same sense of lightness. Of course, it was furnished with antiques, discards of her mother's. Her own sofa was French Provincial in design, covered in a dark brocade. It was stiff and formal, not at all inviting like these furnishings. Had she ever put her feet up on it?

And her apartment building was in an area that her mother approved of. The historic district, of course, one block from her mother's own home, a sprawling eighteenth-century mansion that had been in Emma's family since it had been built.

But the delight Cynthia felt in her space at La Torchere made her suddenly aware of her own apartment's deficiencies. The windows there were small, and the ceilings were too high. There was too much dark oak throughout. The furnishings were not *her,* for all that they were expensive and exquisite.

Here at La Torchere, she didn't know why anyone ever had to go beyond the serenity of their own suite. Cynthia just wished she could have the vacation of her dreams— which was to have three good books to read and the time to read all of them—instead of having to contend with her mother's agenda everyday.

And her mother's agenda was matchmaking. Only the wealthy and successful need apply.

But rather than waste one moment of her hard-fought freedom thinking of that, Cynthia waltzed over to her suitcase and unearthed a well-hidden book that her mother would definitely call trashy. Moments later she had on a pair of comfy pajamas—a long-sleeved top and trouser bottoms. She made herself a cup of cocoa, plumped the pillows on the sofa and settled back with a sigh.

"This is the life," she told herself. Through the doors that opened onto the patio outside her room she could hear the whisper of the sea and the chatter of night birds. A warm, fragrant breeze played across her body. She opened the book and settled into the guilty pleasure of reading all about Jasmine and her sheik.

But rather than soothing her, transporting her to another world, the book seemed to unleash a terrible restlessness in her, a yearning for a life that was not her own. It didn't help that her mother had unearthed the fact that Jerome's granddaughter had met a real live sheik right here at La Torchere, and they had fallen madly in love with each other!

After a few hours of trying desperately to enjoy her fantasy of a perfect evening, Cynthia tossed the book aside. Why was she reading when there was a real world outside her door, exotic and compelling, waiting to be explored?

Not her mother's world of fancy nightclubs and five-star restaurants.

No, Cynthia felt drawn to a world of waves washing sand and flowers releasing their fragrance into the darkness.

She glanced at the clock and snorted.

"At midnight? Cynthia, really." This was happening to her more and more. Even when her mother was not there, it was as if Emma's words issued out of Cynthia's own mouth!

Cynthia got up from the sofa, stepped over the discarded book, and went into the bathroom. She shut the door and studied herself in the mirror. The pajamas—a Christmas gift from her mother—hid whatever shape she had. Her shoulder-length honey-brown hair was pulled back carelessly with an elastic band, her hazel eyes stared back at her unblinkingly through her reading glasses.

"My God, Cyn," she muttered to herself. "When did you

become so pathetic? You are twenty-six years old and frumpy."

Of course, with a little makeup she could highlight the sweep of her cheekbones and the generosity of her mouth. She could make her eyes look green or gold or brown. But why bother?

"Your idea of fun," she reminded herself, " is an evening with a good book. You look exactly like what you are—a research assistant who has never had a real live adventure in her whole life."

Only that wasn't quite true. A long time ago, shrieking with laughter, her arms wrapped around the solid, muscled body of the most beautiful boy in the world, she had ridden behind him on a speeding motorcycle.

His eyes had been the most stunning color of midnight blue, and he'd had the most amazing smile. She'd met him at high school, the high schools in those old districts having an eclectic mix of rich and poor. And he'd been poor. From the wrong side of the tracks, though his humble home had been only a block or two from where she now lived.

It had been years since she'd allowed herself to think of him, and she did not know why she had thought of him now. She brushed away the memory, a tormenting mix of delight and pain.

Still, something lingered and increased her sense of restlessness.

What did a restless person do on this secluded island resort? She had not heard her mother come back yet. Should she go and join them? They would be dancing by now, her mother whirling and twirling like a woman twenty years her junior.

But Cynthia knew that kind of entertainment would not take away the restlessness she was feeling. It might make it worse, make her feel even emptier, as if she was an actress playing a role she could not quite get into.

She left the bathroom and went to the French doors that led outside. She intended to close them, suppress these out-of-character thoughts, cream her face and go to bed.

But with her hand resting on the door handle, she felt the pull of the night. It was incredibly dark out. She could hear the whisper of a restless ocean. And then, as her eyes adjusted to the darkness, she saw thousands of little lights in the sea, bobbing and dancing.

La Torchere had been named for these small phosphorescent sea creatures that lit up the waters around the candelabra-shaped island at night.

But tonight, it seemed those lights dancing playfully in a sea of darkness were calling her name.

"You can't go swimming by yourself in the middle of the night. Alone. It would be reckless."

Her mother's voice, again.

But then Cynthia wondered exactly how reckless it would be. She was a strong swimmer. The only residents of the island were La Torchere's well-heeled guests. In fact, the only way to arrive here was by private ferry or float plane. The employees lived here, too, but all of them seemed charmingly ancient and imminently harmless. The scary people—the kind her mother had warned her about her entire life—were back on the mainland.

If she was going to have an adventure, even a small one, this seemed like it might be the perfect place to indulge herself.

Quickly, before she could change her mind and come to her senses, Cynthia went into her bedroom and put on her bathing suit, an unexciting one-piece high-necked tank suit.

"At least I do have a figure," she muttered to herself, and

then quickly slipped a cover over her body as if just having one was inviting temptations of the sort her mother did not approve.

She turned off all the lights so that if her mother returned to her suite next door she would think her daughter was sleeping. Locking the door behind her, Cynthia made her cautious way down to the flower-scented walkways that led to the beach.

Though late, the air remained as warm as an embrace. The gentle breeze lifted her hair and caressed her skin. The beach was, as she had known it would be, completely deserted. She went to the water's edge, put down her towel, kicked off her shoes, and peeled off the swimsuit cover. The air smelled intoxicating, of the sea, of the night, of mystery.

Cynthia stuck her toe in the water and was greeted by more warmth. It was the first night of the new moon, and the night was so dark she could not tell where the water ended and the sky began.

She was utterly alone, and a new thought came to her. *Skinny dip.*

It was ludicrous.

There was her mother's voice again! But the truth was, Cynthia was not the type of woman who did that kind of thing, though she suddenly found herself pondering the type of woman who did. A rather enticing picture formed in her mind of a woman who was free-spirited, fully engaged in life, adventurous, laughter-filled, not so damned serious, not in the least bit tired or unhappy.

A woman who invited exactly the kind of temptations her mother disapproved of!

Ludicrous, her mother's voice repeated within Cynthia's own mind, and it proved to be the deciding factor.

All right. She would be ludicrous, then, and just a tiny bit reckless. She would give herself this small adventure— this break from convention—as a gift. Tonight, for a few minutes, she would be that free-spirited woman instead of Cynthia Forsythe, professional drudge.

Quickly, before she chickened out, squinting nervously into the impenetrable darkness, Cynthia shed her bathing suit. The night air was astonishing on her naked skin, tender and sensual.

She waded waist-deep and then dove. The water was even better than the air against her nakedness. It was warm and textured, as if she was embraced by liquid silk. Her body felt marvelous, as if it was humming. Cynthia laughed out loud. She became that light-spirited woman of her fantasies as she ducked and dove and swam and played amongst the tiny dancing lights of the sea creatures.

Finally, happy, she flipped on her back and floated in the sea of black—shiny black water meeting inky black sky with no boundary between the two. She imagined she was a star blinking brightly in a universe of darkness.

But she became Cynthia Forsythe again—fell back into her own body with dizzying swiftness—when she heard the slightest sound from the beach.

She lost the relaxation of the float, went under and re-surfaced sputtering, her eyes stinging from salt water and her mouth full of the bitter taste. Warily, she turned her attention beachward.

She saw the distinctive flaring of a match, and then the glowing red tip of a cigarette. No, a cigar. The pungent aroma floated out over the darkness to her, rich and spicy.

Women didn't generally smoke cigars, so unless she was mistaken there was a man on that beach! And here she was cavorting around, nude.

Completely vulnerable, her mother's voice informed her with a little *tsk* of satisfaction. This was where heeding the call of adventure led: to the unpredictable, to trouble, to danger.

Cynthia forced herself to think. She could swim farther up the shore and get out of the water, but unfortunately her clothes were on the beach. She did not relish a long walk through the privileged enclaves of La Torchere without a stitch of clothing.

Her other option was to wait, and that she did, but the minutes dragged by, and even after the light of the cigar had been extinguished, she could see a dark shape still on the beach. Her eyes had now adjusted enough to the darkness that the outline told her quite a bit about this unexpected intruder. He was definitely masculine, definitely powerful, infinitely formidable.

Did he know she was there? Had he heard her? Had he seen her bathing suit and cover and towel and shoes?

The best-case scenario was that the resolution of this situation was going to be embarrassing, and the worst-case scenario was that it would become very dangerous.

"Cynthia Forsythe," she chided herself inwardly, her teeth beginning to chatter. "You should have known you were the least likely person to have an adventure!"

Rick Barnett had come to love the night. It protected him from people's curious stares, but it was more than that.

Almost in compensation for the damage to his left eye, his right one had developed quite amazing nocturnal vision. At night, it felt as though he had a sixth sense that warned him of obstacles before he even saw them. It wasn't perfect, he still had a tendency to bash himself on his blind left side, but it was better than during the day, when he often felt he was listing crazily, unbalanced and uneasy with his restricted vision.

Tonight, he had come to scout sites for the chapel. Ms. Montrose, that strange old woman with a young woman's eyes, an astonishing color of blue-violet, had mentioned a number of possible locations to him, but he had checked them all out and none had spoken to him.

Perhaps accepting the commission to design and build a wedding chapel had been a mistake.

He was a cynical man by nature. He had been even before the accident that had blinded him, laid waste to half his face, and crushed his larynx so that his voice was a harsh growl, almost animallike. Now he was more so, particularly given how rapidly the female of the species assessed the damage to his face and ran the other way. Six months since the accident. His calendar was empty; the lights on his message machine did not blink; his phone did not ring. He had been seeing a woman, fairly seriously, at the time of the accident. She had abandoned ship and when he looked at himself in the mirror he did not blame her.

The doctors told him that eventually the scarring would fade and he would learn to compensate for the loss of half his vision.

Eventually.

There would be no repair for his voice.

Meanwhile, the accident had left him even more hardened than he had been before, only now he wasn't even attractive. So, he certainly did not believe in anything as ethereal as happily-ever-after.

The truth was, Rick Barnett was not sure what he believed in anymore.

As if his life didn't feel hellish enough, he'd had to spot Cynthia Forsythe at this very resort? What were the chances of that? The gods seemed to be having quite a good chuckle at his expense!

Once he would have loved to run into her, the girl who had scorned his high-school advances because he was from the wrong side of the tracks. Once he would have loved to introduce her to some of the old-money beauties who clung to his arm and stared into his face as if they could not get enough of him.

But now? He did not want to see Cynthia. He hoped she'd be leaving La Torchere soon and their paths would not cross before that happened.

Rick found himself on a bluff, a rocky outcropping west of the beach, and the hair raised suddenly on the back of his neck. This place did not have the manicured feel of the rest of the resort. It had been left natural. A place of rocks and trees, the landscape rugged and untamed.

He was not sure how he knew, but he knew. This was it. This was where the chapel would go. Was it hypocritical for a man who had no belief in romance, nor in the power of love, to build a wedding chapel?

Probably.

And yet, as he stood here, on this piece of ground, he could almost feel the chapel forming around him. The spirit of it, for no vision of the building itself came to him. He just knew he would put it here, on this rock bluff, facing the sea and all its mysteries.

He loved to build. That did not mean he had to believe in love.

A beautiful, carefree feminine laugh floated over the night air. The hackles on the back of his neck rose again. It was almost as though the gods were laughing at his refusal to believe in love.

It was nonsense, of course. When he walked to the edge

of the bluff, he could see the water rippling around a woman who was swimming, alone, in the bay. She laughed again, and the sound tickled along his spine.

Good God. Cynthia?

He would know her laugh anywhere. He had heard it, the robust joyousness of it, a long time ago when she had had her cheek pressed hard into the black leather of his jacket, when her arms had been curled tight around him.

For a moment, he could taste the bitterness of her rejection, and it combined with all the other rejections he had received recently.

He squinted at her, her body a pool of light in a sea of darkness. Those unusual, glow-in-the-dark sea creatures lit the water around her so that it looked as though she was swimming in the sky, not the ocean.

That sixth sense, so finely honed, filled in what he could not see. Cynthia-Miss-Snooty-Forsythe was swimming in the buff.

It was childish and vindictive, and Rick Barnett didn't give a damn. It was payback time. For her snub of him, for all the snubs of beautiful women who now found him unworthy, he was exacting revenge. Nothing major. Small but satisfying.

He made his way off the bluff to the beach. It was even better than he thought. Her clothes were in an untidy bundle on the sand. If he was not mistaken, her bathing suit— black and proper, exactly what the Cynthia he had known would wear—was on the top of the heap.

He propped himself up against a huge piece of driftwood that had washed in and took his time preparing and lighting the cigar.

She noticed him right away, the movement in the water suddenly stilled. Though it was very dark out, he could see the white roundness of her head bobbing as she trod water and tried to think what to do.

He let her think, never letting on that he knew she was there.

He took his time with the cigar, but even so, she said nothing, hoping to outwait him. He laughed to himself at that and put out the cigar. He crossed his arms over his chest. No one could outwait a man who had all the time in the world.

Finally her voice called out, tremulous.

He frowned at the faint tremor. He'd meant to embarrass her, not scare her. On the other hand, maybe she was just cold.

"Excuse me?" she called.

"Yes?" he answered back.

The growl was not what she was expecting, because she was silent for a moment, contemplating. Then she continued.

"You've caught me at an awkward moment. Do you think you could leave the beach while I get out of the water?"

"No." Had he known her own delight in the power of that word only hours before, he might have said it again.

Her attempt at politeness vanished. "A gentleman would."

"I'm not a gentleman," Rick assured her, and the rasp of his voice backed him up. In fact these days when he looked in the mirror, a pirate looked back at him, battle-scarred and hard. Miss Snobby would be swimming the other way if she had any idea.

"Look, it would be a shame if I had to report you to the authorities."

He smiled at that. Authorities on Torchere Key? But the

smile faded. She had that same note in her voice that he had always remembered. Blue-blooded. Used to being listened to. Her pronunciation perfect.

"Report me to the authorities?" he said. "I'm enjoying a quiet moment on the beach, perfectly attired, I might add. You're the one out there with nothing on."

He heard her gasp.

"How do you know?" she snapped. "It's dark!"

Despite her combative tone, he heard the plea in her words, and the prayer. She was hoping he hadn't seen her. Was she every bit the same Miss Priss she had been? Impossible. She was twenty-six years old now. Some man, somewhere, had tasted the honey of her lips, brought all that leashed passion to the surface.

He didn't want to think about that, so he walked over to the bundle of her clothes and lifted them with his toe. "Your suit is here on the beach. And some sort of shift. And a towel." He studied the suit more closely than he had the first time, and then the shift underneath it. Cynthia had always had a glorious body, slender, but round in all the right places.

The suit, and the hideous shift, did not look like clothing that belonged to a woman who had come into herself, found her passion.

Had she married? The thought brought unexpected pain, like a knife going through his heart. *She might have three children by now, for all he knew.*

He told himself the ache in his heart was only because it would be so unfair if she had gone on to find happiness when his life was in such shambles. He would just find out, that was all. He'd find out, and then he'd fade back into the night, where he had become so comfortable.

"I'll make you a deal," he said.

"I'll hear what you have to say."

He found it faintly amusing that she wasn't giving an inch even though she was in no position to bargain.

"I'll turn my back while you come out of the water and get wrapped up in a towel."

"Is that your best offer?"

At least she didn't sound afraid. Madder than a wet hen, but not afraid.

"Actually, there's more. I'll turn my back in exchange for something."

Her silence was long. "What?" she finally asked.

It was his silence that was long this time, as he contemplated what he was about to ask her. "A kiss," he finally said.

"Are you insane?" she sputtered.

"Maybe."

Again the silence was long. "What kind of kiss?" she asked, finally.

"How many kinds are there?" he asked back.

"There's the gentle, kiss-on-the-cheek kind." She sounded extremely hopeful.

"That wasn't quite what I had in mind," he said drily.

"There's the little buss on the lips kind."

"Getting closer." This exchange was already revealing an amazing fact to him. She was still the innocent girl she had been, her passion leashed, subdued. If she were married, she'd had plenty of opportunity to tell him she was going to sic her husband on him.

"You are not engaging me in a wet, sloppy kiss! You are a complete stranger. And you've been smoking a cigar."

Cynthia Forsythe was twenty-six years old and she thought kissing was wet and sloppy? And she sounded more concerned about the cigar than the fact he was a stranger.

"Take it or leave it," he said, and he turned his back. "I'm counting to twenty, and then I'm turning around."

"Oh! You are impossible. This is absurd."

"One…two…three…"

Her griping came to an abrupt end and he could hear her moving strongly through the water. His diminished vision had heightened some of his other senses, and so he could tell by the sounds exactly where she was. At the water's edge, coming up the beach, grabbing her clothes. It took a will of absolute iron to not turn and take a small peek.

Her scent caught him. She was right behind him. She smelled of the sea, but also sweet and clean. Delicious.

She could, of course, pick up her clothes and run, but she didn't. He heard her struggling into them, the dry cloth catching on her wet skin.

"All right," she said regally. "You may turn around."

"Close your eyes," he ordered her softly.

"Humph. No description for the authorities."

He turned and looked. Her eyes were obediently screwed closed. She was beautiful up close, her face unmarred by life. Her cheekbones were high; her small nose tilted regally toward the heavens. Her wet hair was plastered against her head, the color of dark gold. It would be lighter in color when it was dry, in the sunlight, and for some reason he was pleased that it was not full of the streaks and dyes dictated by current fashion.

The swimsuit cover was not anything dictated by current fashion either. It looked much worse on than it had off. It had the shape and style and coloring of a gunny sack. But it was clinging delightfully to some of her wetter curves. Her figure was slightly fuller than it had been, and it reminded him she was a woman now, not a girl.

It reminded him he did not know her at all. Not now.

But her mouth was as glorious a creation as he had remembered, generous, the bottom lip plump and full.

"What would you report, anyway?" he asked her, softly, trying to strip some of the harshness from his voice. "A kiss bandit?"

"Just get it over with," she said icily. "And if you taste like cigars, I'll probably puke on your shoes."

He gazed at her a moment longer and then leaned toward her. He touched her lips with his own.

He tasted the sweetness and innocence that he had suspected from her earlier words. And despite her claim that she would be repelled by the lingering taste of the cigar on his lips, her mouth remained soft underneath his, pliable, almost inviting.

How could she be both? Sweet and innocent? And yet inviting a deeper kiss with a strange man?

"Will your husband be coming to even the score with me?" he asked. He had to *know*. It wasn't enough to guess.

"I'm not married," she said, and her voice held the quiver of that kiss. "I've never been married."

"Ah."

He pulled back from her, saw her eyes begin to flutter open and resisted the urge to see them once again. Her eyes had been her glory, a mix of gold and green and brown that was intoxicating. He covered them quickly with his palm.

"Good night, sweet lady," he said, turned swiftly and walked quickly away through the sand.

He had accomplished nothing that he had set out to, least of all revenge. He felt terribly unsettled by the touch of her lips, by this midnight encounter with an old love.

He turned on the edge of the palm-lined walk that went back toward the main resort and looked back at her.

She stood frozen in the night, a hand lifted to her lips.

A faint breeze had kicked up, and the swim cover was molded to the beautiful ripeness of her breasts, the strong, slender length of her upper legs. Strands of her wet hair lifted and whipped around the soft profile of her lovely face. In dark silhouette, she looked like a goddess who had walked out of the sea.

The scars on his face ached, a painful and ruthless reminder that he was the man least likely to have anything to offer a goddess.

Chapter Two

Cynthia stood, her hand to her lips, looking at the empty space where the darkness had swallowed the stranger. He had disappeared completely, almost reminding her of how wild creatures could melt into invisibility.

The wind off the ocean caressed her wet body and lifted the heaviness of her hair. She felt a wonderful surging power, as if she were a goddess standing on that beach embraced by darkness.

"Wild creatures and goddesses," she muttered derisively, broken from her trance. She stooped to pick up her towel. Still, she felt reluctant to leave the image of herself as a woman of such seductive powers that she could tempt a perfectly sane man into participating in that encounter.

Because for all that it had been bizarre, she had been left with a sense that he was not. His lips, when they had touched hers, had not been hard or grasping. The kiss had not been creepy. In fact, far from it. His lips had told her secrets. They had told her he was a man of solidness and strength, a man who did not make it a habit to kiss strangers on the beach.

"Cynthia," she told herself primly, "you did not lure!" For heaven's sake, she had been accosted by a complete barbarian. Why was she making excuses for him? Who in this day and age demanded a kiss in return for civilized behavior?

And got away with it, she reminded herself with an attempt at stern disapproval.

The problem was that she didn't feel the least little bit accosted. Try as she might, Cynthia could not seem to whip herself into the frenzy of indignation the encounter deserved! She had just come away from a bad deal with the devil. She had actually agreed to trade a kiss for a moment's privacy. The man was a pirate.

"I've been victimized," she told herself, kicking up the sand looking for her shoes. The words totally lacked conviction. If she was honest, she would admit it felt as though she was trying to manufacture the way her mother would have wanted her to feel.

She gave up the search for the shoes and headed across the sand toward the beautiful twisting pathway that would lead her through an exotic world of tropical plants back to the safety of her room. But rather than hurrying back to that sanctuary, she found herself dawdling. She was aware of how delightful the sand felt squishing up between her toes and then of the warmth seeping through the pavement into her bare feet. She was aware of the scent of the night, the sea smell mixed with the wild abundance of colorful and aromatic flowers that bloomed in well-groomed beds. Most of all, she was aware of the night air on her cool, damp skin, sensuous as a touch.

He had touched her, the palm of his hand rough and

masculine against the softness of her cheek as he had guided her lips to his.

Why hadn't she pulled away?

"A deal's a deal," she told herself righteously, "even if it is with the devil."

But she knew she was lying to herself. She had not lingered over that kiss on the flimsy excuse that she had made a deal. No, she had been drawn into the unsavory deal because his mouth had tasted faintly of cigars, and, unlike her vow, the taste had not given her the least desire to upchuck on his shoes.

No, there had been nothing repelling about the taste on his firm lips—smokey and faintly sweet—like perfectly aged port wine. And his kiss had been that rich, that intoxicating, that compelling.

From the moment her lips had touched his, the world she knew had faded away, replaced with a far different one. A world of hammering hearts, of sweet-tasting lips, of a scent so masculine it could be bottled and sold. She had entered, without warning, a world of *wanting,* as unfamiliar and exotic to her as visiting a foreign land. Yet that world had opened to her with the hesitant parting of her lips beneath the command of his.

"That's a little much to read into one kiss," she told herself, but even as she said it, she knew her world was already altered. When was the last time she had felt the simple joy of bare feet on warm pavement, felt night air tingle against her skin like a lover's touch? Not just noticed it, but *felt* it, as if her eyes and her pores and her heart were suddenly wide open?

Cynthia felt alive.

"Like a sleeping princess awakened by a kiss," she whispered to the night and then snorted at her fancifulness. Goddesses. Princesses. Pirates. Wild creatures.

Obviously her life had become just a little too dull and predictable. She slid in the door of her suite, noting, thankfully, that her mother had not returned to the room next door. Her mother had a gift for *knowing* things she had no business knowing.

Her back against the door, Cynthia closed her eyes. Her senses were filled with the taste of him and the smell of him once more. She *yearned*.

"Stop it," she ordered herself, appalled. She pushed off from the door and then noticed the book she had left open on the couch.

Hot Desert Kisses, it was called. Jasmine and the sheik. Did Cynthia have to look any further than her reading material for the reason she was feeling this way? All hot and bothered and unfulfilled? Her mother was right. This type of book was trashy. And it led to all kinds of ridiculous fantasies. Reading this could lead to nothing but restlessness and discontent. No wonder that kiss had affected her so terribly! With stony determination, she plopped the book into the garbage can.

Then Cynthia went into her bedroom, peeled off the damp swimsuit and stared at the shapeless pants and jacket of the pajamas she had taken off just a short while ago. The design had rabbits in it! Had she ever noticed that before? She studied the pajamas with distaste. Cute bunnies with mischievous eyes and pink bows and ridiculously large feet cavorted all over her sleepwear!

In the last hour she had made three rather startling discoveries about herself: She liked walking barefoot in warm sand; she liked swimming naked in the night; and she would die to be kissed like that again! She was not the kind of woman who wore bunny pajamas to bed!

In bed, moments later, clad in a T-shirt and underwear,

Cynthia talked sense to herself. "So, you need a new pair of pajamas," she scolded herself, "and maybe a new hobby. Something you can feel excited about. Photography. Bird-watching."

Not quite, a voice inside her insisted, something *exciting*.

"Okay, then, skateboarding. Downhill skiing."

Nope.

"Skydiving. Bungee-jumping."

But the voice inside her said *hot tropical kisses.*

"Shut up," she told the voice firmly.

But just before she slept, she thought she heard a voice, rough as a gravel road, scraping along her spine and making her skin feel hot and tender.

Good night, sweet lady.

"Good night," she murmured.

The next thing she knew she was awake, and it was morning. She was drenched in the peach-colored light of post dawn. Cynthia lay very still, contemplating the deep sense of delight within her. When was the last time she had awoken feeling like this? With this kind of tingling anticipation for what the day might hold? With a strange desire to embrace the unexpected?

She was probably never going to see that man again, Cynthia reminded herself sharply. Or encounter him. "Seeing" him was stretching the experience a bit.

She was becoming an old maid—desperate and pathetic—building dream castles out of a ridiculous and demeaning encounter that any woman with an ounce of good sense would have found insulting!

If she ever encountered that man again, what was she going to do? Swoon? Of course not! She would never give him the satisfaction of knowing the chaos and confusion he had stirred up inside her. She would be cool. Composed. Icy, even. Daring him to steal another kiss…

A knock came on her door, and she pulled a pillow over her head, not willing to encounter the real world.

But then the possibility entered her head that, now that her life had expanded to include the potential for unpredictable moments, it might actually be him!

What if he had tracked her down, as enthralled and intrigued by that kiss as she had been? What if he stood outside her door, with a bouquet of red roses and an apologetic smile on his face? She'd let him have a piece of her mind…before she forgave him.

Cynthia flew from the bed, tugged a hand through the tangle of her hair, tossed a housecoat over her T-shirt and panties and stormed to the door.

She threw it open, and no one was there.

Fantasy collided abruptly and painfully with reality when she realized the knock was coming from the door that adjoined her suite to her mother's.

Trying to bite back her disappointment, resigned, she opened that door. Her mother stood there, perfectly coiffed, not looking the least as if she had danced the night away.

"Darling, time for breakfast."

"You don't eat breakfast," Cynthia reminded her mother, shocked. "Mother, you are never up before the crack of noon."

"Baron Gunterburger—Wilhelm—talked me into joining him. He was so disappointed that you couldn't join us last night. He left early, but made me promise to drag you along to breakfast."

Her mother stopped abruptly and studied her daughter. One eyebrow shot up and her lips pursed thoughtfully.

"What on earth have you been up to?"

"Excuse me? I just got out of bed." Why did she feel

guilty? As if she *had* been up to something? Was there a law against fantasizing about the man who had kissed you showing up at your door to ply you with roses, apologies and promises? Well, probably in her mother's world. There were rules about everything in her mother's world!

"That's just it. It's not like you to sleep late, and," her mother's eyes narrowed, "you have a look about you."

"A look?" Cynthia asked with feigned innocence.

"You don't have pajamas on. You aren't naked under that housecoat, are you?"

"Mother!"

"Well, you look as if you've just been, er, tumbled."

"Tumbled?" Cynthia repeated, nonplused. "Tumbled?"

Her mother looked her up and down and then asked softly, shocked, "Is there someone in there with you?"

She was twenty-six years old. Her mother knew as well as anyone else that there was *never* anyone with her. But instead of reassuring her mother, she wished she had the nerve to tell her it was none of her business. She wished she was the woman who had swum naked last night, because that woman would have men in her bedroom at dawn if she damn well pleased!

Instead, Cynthia found herself stepping back from the door, so her mother could see through the suite to the open bedroom door and her rumpled—and very empty—bed.

"Well, then, you look as if you wish you'd been, er, tumbled." This was said as if wishing for it was just as great a crime as having done it.

"Tumbled," Cynthia muttered. "What is that? Some seventeenth-century term you've been waiting for an opportunity to use?"

Still, she turned away before her mother could see the

blush she could feel burning in her own cheeks. She looked at the clock and gave a theatrical little squeak.

"I have overslept, haven't I?" she said, forcing a breezy note into her voice. "I'll meet you for breakfast in fifteen. Save me a place beside the baron."

If there was one way to distract her mother, it was to play her game.

It worked. Her mother cooed with startled pleasure. "You won't be sorry. You're going to love him, Cynthia."

So love was okay, and probably tumbling, too, as long as the suitor was mommy-approved. Her own cynicism took her by surprise. As she got ready, she managed to salvage a tiny bit of the enthusiasm she had first felt this morning by entertaining a fantasy just as probable as red roses and apologies.

What if it was him? What if the baron was the mystery man who had kissed her last night? Her mother had said he'd left early. Had he wandered down to the beach?

Not that she had detected even a trace of an accent. But then wasn't it possible that a wealthy, well-traveled, well-educated German might speak without an accent? Maybe the raspiness of that voice had been a disguise.

She remembered that voice with a shiver. A voice made of gravel and silk. Impossibly sexy, utterly masculine.

An hour later Cynthia wondered if her mother might have been right.

What was not to love about the singularly handsome and charming young baron? If she had met him twenty-four hours ago, would she have considered him?

He was blond. He had intense blue eyes and a perfect cut of feature. He was casually, but tastefully, dressed, tan and extremely athletic looking.

But he was most definitely not the man she had met last night. She had known before she had even heard him speak, known as soon as she had seen him sharing the table with her mother as she entered the restaurant.

She was not sure how she had been so certain, but she had felt the ache of deep disappointment, which she was willing to admit was a funny reaction given the fact that if it had been her mystery man, she fully intended to greet him by slapping him across the face!

"You're as lovely as your mother promised," the baron said, giving her the full wattage of his smile.

Cynthia was pretty sure the young woman at the next table nearly fainted when he bent over Cynthia's hand and placed a kiss on it.

It was a gesture of such old-world courtliness that she really should have appreciated it. Instead, she snuck a quick look around the room. The man from last night could be anyone here! He could be watching her right now! She felt a tingle of excitement as she contemplated that possibility.

The baron pulled back her chair, and over the next hour proved himself to be attentive, witty and charming.

To Cynthia, despite his considerable charm, the baron did not seem quite real.

She was not sure how it was possible that a man who had emerged from the shadows and then melted back into them, who had been far more dream than reality, could seem so much more real than the handsome flesh-and-blood man vying so nobly and sweetly for her attention.

She found herself scanning the restaurant over and over again, hoping to see someone who would be familiar in some way. In what way she wasn't quite sure. She had not even seen the face of the man who had claimed her lips last night.

But as he had walked away, leaving her lips still tingling from the sensuousness of his kiss, she had seen the dark silhouette of his powerful build, been captivated by his grace, had been left with the sensation she would know him anywhere.

Restless thoughts stirred within her. Was she ever going to see him again? How? It felt as if she had to see him again, as if she could be returned to the sleeping state she had been locked in for so many years if she did not see him again.

Suddenly the baron and her mother seemed like a trap, a trap that would return her to that state of not quite living that she had accepted for far too long.

"Excuse me," she said abruptly. "I just thought of something I have to do."

"Nonsense," her mother said, blinking at her with sweet warning. "Everything you have to do is for me, and we have nothing so urgent that we can't spend a few more minutes with our charming companion."

Cynthia stared at her mother, but she was seeing something else.

A young girl—herself—leaning over the bed of her dying father.

"Promise me," he whispered, his last words, "Cynthia, promise me."

"What?" she asked desperately. "Anything."

"I've brought her nothing but unhappiness," he said sadly.

They both knew he meant her mother. It had been a marriage made in hell, the spell of her father's great looks soon waning in the face of his desperate unsuitability for her mother's blue-blooded world.

"Cynthia, always look after her. Make her happy."

She had promised, and it was that simple. Had it been a hard promise to keep? Yes. But duty came before passion. Those were the rules in the real world, the rules of her mother's world.

There had been a boy in high school who had tested that

resolve, from the wrong side of the tracks, as surely as her father had been. She could still remember the way her arms had felt wrapped around the leather of his jacket as she rode the back of his motorcycle.

She could still remember his name.

Rick Barnett.

Her mother had found out about him and had ordered her to end it. And she had. Cynthia had witnessed firsthand her mother and father's exhausting and impossible efforts to marry two worlds. But more, Rick had brought out a wild side she would have been just as pleased not to make acquaintance with. That long-ago boy had brought her to the edge of her self-control—

"Cynthia," her mother said sharply, bringing her back to earth. "Quit looking at me like that, as though you've seen a ghost."

She felt as if she *had* seen a ghost. What had made her think of Rick, now, after all these years? When the pain of that loss finally had seemed dull and a long, long way away?

The baron's hand covered Cynthia's, and he smiled at her. "On the other hand, my dear, you may look at me any way you choose."

Her mother giggled. "Oh, how utterly lovely you are, Wilhelm."

Cynthia snatched her hand away, feeling oddly as though she had been unfaithful by letting another man touch her. She leapt up from the table.

"Really," she said, "I must go."

"But I was just going to ask Wilhelm to tell you about his yacht. That's how he arrived here at La Torchere. He's moored—"

Cynthia scrambled away, not even glancing back when her mother called after her indignantly.

She knew exactly where she was going and she didn't stop until she arrived back at the beach that had enticed her last night.

It looked different in the day. A scene off a postcard of a perfect vacation—white sands reaching out to turquoise waters, palm trees swaying in a light breeze—but something essential was missing. The magic. The mystery.

Cynthia settled on a lovely wrought-iron bench that had been placed strategically at the sand's edge overlooking the beach. She looked out over the tranquil waters, jade-shaded in the early morning light, trying to recapture something of what she had felt last night. Was it possible she had dreamed it?

Her gaze stopped on a large rock protruding from the tranquil waters of the cove and her breath caught in her throat. Something of what she was looking for—the essence of her experience—was in that rock.

Had it been there last night?

Had it been there before?

Of course it had to have been there! Huge rocks didn't just appear in the water off the shore. The rock had the shape and size of a bear, massive and restless, the power unmistakable.

"Hello, my dear."

Cynthia glanced up, startled to find she was no longer alone. A woman she recognized vaguely from the resort's front office was standing beside the bench, one hand resting on it, her eyes fastened on the rock.

Despite her stylish dress, the woman bore an unfortunate resemblance to the wicked witch in *Snow White,* but when she turned her eyes to Cynthia, Cynthia saw a startling beauty in them. They were an astonishing shade of violet.

"Has that rock always been there?" she asked, even though it seemed a foolish question. "I can't believe I never noticed it before."

"Oh." The woman waved her hand dismissively. "You know. The tides."

Of course. The tides would come and go, revealing things and hiding things with the water's changing depths.

"Could I join you for a moment?"

Considering how eager she had been to divest herself of her mother's and the baron's company, Cynthia felt strangely open to sharing her bench with the old woman.

"Merry Montrose," the woman said, extending her hand.

Cynthia was startled by the handshake. There was nothing old about it. In fact she felt a shiver of pure energy run up and down her arm as she accepted the woman's hand.

"Cynthia Forsythe."

"Yes, I know."

Cynthia looked askance.

"Resort manager. I try to keep abreast of who is here. Are you enjoying your stay with us?"

"It's a beautiful place," Cynthia said, since enjoyment was not quite how she would describe the unsettled feelings within her.

"Ah, yes," Ms. Montrose said, "the mixed joy of vacationing with family. Nothing against your mother, of course. I enjoy her writing immensely."

Cynthia grinned as if she had found a conspirator. But in what?

"Is that a pair of shoes out there in the sand?"

"I believe it is," Cynthia said, spotting her missing sandals half buried under a mound of sand.

"Oh," Merry said happily. "Do you suppose there was a romantic tryst here last night?"

Cynthia looked at her warily. Had there been more than just the two of them, then?

But Merry had switched her attention from the shoes. "The rock always reminds me of a story, a legend, a gift from our Native American ancestors. Would you like me to tell it to you?"

Cynthia felt a strange shiver. It was one of those moments when you knew the decision you were about to make had repercussions you did not fully understand, but that changed your life forever.

Far too strong a reaction for an old woman's offer to share a tale.

But then weren't all her reactions slightly out of kilter right now, because of the power and mystery of a kiss stolen after midnight? It was as if a spell had been cast on her.

"I would like to hear the story." She was aware even as she said the words that she felt as though she had no choice, she was on a collision course with destiny.

Merry patted her hand, as if she understood the underlying tension. Her voice was soothing and melodious, not the voice of an old woman.

"This is a story from the Native people of the Northwest Coast. Do you know that area? The coastline of British Columbia, running all the way up to Alaska?"

Cynthia shook her head, no.

"It is a narrow, untamed belt of temperate rainforest. It embraces about twelve-hundred miles of rugged coastline, and rocky islands and inlets. It is a place of extreme rainfall and dense mist, where the cedar trees grow to unimaginable size in the shadows of the Coast and Rocky Mountains. It is a place of vibrant greens and formidable and mystical grays.

"The mists," she said, almost dreamily. "They make

anything seem possible. The line between shore and water, mountain and tree fades, blurs, until it is hard to know what is real and what is not."

In Cynthia's mind, she could see the place Merry described, feel the brooding mystery of it, almost as if her own line between what was in her mind and what was real was blurring.

"This is a story from the Tsimshian people. It is called 'The Bear Who Married a Woman.'"

Cynthia shivered, because the rock had so reminded her of a bear, but also because she had come back to the beach seeking some of the essence of what she had felt last night. She had not found what she sought.

Until she had seen the rock.

She settled back on the bench, her eyes fastened on the "bear" as she listened to the soft soothing sound of a master storyteller weaving a tale.

"In the time before the great sadness came upon the people—when they carved the totem poles and the great canoes, and celebrated the potlatch and the sacredness of dance, in the time before their children were stolen from their own homes—the People of the Tsimshian lived traditionally by the ocean and gloried in abundance.

"There was a widow who had a beautiful daughter who was modest and hardworking. The daughter wove extraordinary cedar baskets and mats, and she lived with the chastity and purity that were sacred among the tribes. Her black hair swung past her waist, and her dark eyes were lit with the light of the sun upon water. She was much sought after as a wife and many a young man tried to woo her, but she declined them all.

"Her mother had given her precise instructions. 'When a man comes to marry you, feel the palms of his hands.

If they are soft, send him away, but if they are rough, accept him.'"

Cynthia remembered the roughness of the palm on her cheek last night and gasped out loud at this strange parallel between the story and what had happened to her last night. But Merry appeared lost in the telling of the tale and did not pause, did not even appear to have heard her.

"The widow in her wisdom wanted a good man for her daughter, not one who was lazy, but one who worked hard and knew the traditional ways, whose hands were rough from building canoes and hauling nets, from holding the spear above the surfacing whale."

Cynthia thought her own mother would want qualities that were quite different. The hard hands of a working man would not be on her list of desired qualities of a suitor for her daughter!

"The daughter obeyed her mother. She rejected the wooing of many young men. But one night a youth came to her bed. In the darkness, she could not see him, but when his hand took hers she felt the roughness of it, and her heart gladdened. She accepted him and gave him the gift of herself.

"But in the morning, when she woke, her new husband was gone. She had not even seen his face. But her mother found a halibut on the beach right in front of their lodge, even though it was midwinter, not the time halibut graced these waters.

"The following evening, cloaked in darkness, the husband returned to his young wife. Again, he left before first light, and again he left a gift for his mother-in-law and his new wife, this time a seal. The newlyweds lived like this for some time. The young woman never saw the face of her husband, but each morning she found an offering on the beach, and each morning it was larger than the time before.

Thus the mother and her daughter became rich by the standards of the People. They had abundant food. They had oil. They had hides from seals left by the new husband.

"The widow was anxious to see her son-in-law, and one day she waited until he arrived. At dusk, she saw a red bear emerge from the water. He carried a whale on either side and put them down on the beach. But as soon as he noticed he was being watched, he was transformed into a rock. He had been a supernatural creature from the sea."

Cynthia stared out at the rock, knowing what Merry's next words would be before she said them.

"Which can be seen up to this day by the person with the right heart."

Cynthia felt shivers going up and down her spine because of her encounter the night before—kissed by an unknown assailant—who had vanished into the night, with the stealth of a wild creature.

The silence stretched between her and Merry.

"So," her companion asked her, finally, gently, "did you like my story?"

Cynthia hesitated. She could be diplomatic and just say yes. Instead, she heard herself saying, "I found it very unsettling."

"Really? Why?"

"He turns into a rock at the end? What kind of story is that?" She heard more emotion in her voice than should have been there. It was only a story! But she looked out at the rock and felt uneasy at how much it did look like a bear frozen in time.

Merry laughed softly. "Ah, yes, most cultures prefer a linear style to a story. In other words, it follows a line, in order—beginning, middle and end. And naturally the end is supposed to be happily ever after."

Having been her mother's assistant for so many years, Cynthia knew the mechanics of telling a story. Naturally it had a beginning, a middle and an end! She liked the happily-ever-after part, too, though her mother's missives were generally a little too dry for that.

"There's another way to tell stories?" she demanded, feeling strangely threatened by this encounter, her second odd one in as many days. She had spent her entire life not having odd encounters, and now she was attracting them like bees to honey!

"Native people tend to think in a circle," Ms. Montrose told her patiently, "so there is not always a readily discernible beginning, middle and end to their stories."

Cynthia found herself intrigued. "What do you mean? I don't understand that."

"The Native people often tell stories that do not give easy answers. Instead, they engage the listener and ask them to find their own truths within the context of the story, to explore their own relationships with the elements that appear in the story, and then either to embrace or reject the lesson.

"Of course, back then, part of the purpose of the story would have been to define the responsibilities and duties of the people in the tribe."

"She married a bear!" Cynthia said. "That doesn't seem like a definition of duty!"

"The natives of that area often have human-animal ancestors as part of their storytelling. They associate profound spirit powers with animals, those powers give supernatural protection."

"So was it a good thing she married a bear?"

"Perhaps love always lifts us up to a place of the supernatural," Merry suggested.

"Then why did he turn into a rock?"

"If you play with the tale inside your own head, perhaps things will become clearer to you."

"That seems very complicated. I wouldn't even know where to begin. Or why I would want to."

"Start with one element of the story," Merry suggested, just as if Cynthia had not questioned why she would want to! "Begin with the bear. Ask yourself what the bear means to you."

Feeling as if she'd been given an unwanted homework assignment, Cynthia watched, bemused, as Merry got up and walked away, her step the light one of a much younger woman.

"Weird," she muttered in an effort to brush the whole thing off, one that failed. She waited until Merry was out of sight, retrieved her shoes and then went back to her suite, contemplating the strange encounter.

What did the bear mean to her? She knew very little about bears.

But she did know they were creatures of the night.

And that knowledge made her shiver. What would it hurt to find out a little bit more? To accept this odd challenge she had been given? To stretch a bit out of her comfort zone?

She spent the afternoon on the Internet, curling her bare feet into the sensuous pile of the room's carpet and finding out more about bears than she thought there was to know. And trying very hard not to do two things: not to convince herself that she had been kissed by a bear the night before and not to fantasize about a knock on the door from a man standing there with roses, apologies and promises lighting the wicked depths of eyes she somehow knew would be dark as night.

Chapter Three

The day was fading. Rick sat on the ground with his back braced by the rough trunk of a tree with spreading branches that provided shade for this whole glade. He was sketching furiously, trying to get this latest idea down before the light failed him. He sat in a litter of balled-up sketches that had not satisfied him, and he knew, even as he reached for it, that this last effort would be no better than the ones that had come before it.

It was a coincidence, nothing more, that he could see the crescent of beach where he had waylaid Cynthia the night before. Still, it was an uncomfortable coincidence. He was not sure what rebel had surfaced within him and made that deal with her, but if he had set out to punish her, to seek revenge for a long-ago slight, he had succeeded only in unsettling himself.

Every whiff of flower- and sea-scented air made him remember. The strawberry taste of her lips, her alabaster skin, her delectable wet curves pressed into the swim-suit cover.

So stunned had he been by what her kiss had unleashed in him that he had forgotten his agenda. He had set out on a mission to exact revenge for all the beautiful women who had rejected him and who would reject him in the future.

He had never expected to be kissed back!

Now he thought of all the things he wished he had asked her while he'd held her captive. What did she do now? Had she become the great artist that she had once dreamed of being?

Not, he thought wryly, that she would have answered him. Not the Cynthia he remembered. She would have pointed her little blue-blooded nose at the heavens and told him it was none of his business.

Her kiss hinted at innocence, as if she had not pro-gressed in passion since the twelfth grade.

Was that even possible? And why did he care?

The more pressing question was, would she come back tonight, lured here by a sliver of moonlight and a hint of mystery?

It was the question he had been trying to outrun all day, but no matter how furiously he sketched, resketched, pon-dered and sketched again, the question continued to tickle the back of his mind.

Would she come back to the beach tonight? And if she did, what would it mean?

And what about him? The truth was he was already here, watching. Waiting? What would he do if she came back?

"Walk away, if you have an ounce of sense." But he thought it might take a stronger man than him to walk away from Cynthia. He heard again the musical lilt of her laughter as she had cavorted in the water, naked, thinking she was alone.

"I should have looked when I had the chance," he said. "I might not get another."

He put a furious line through the roof he had just drawn, changed it, angled it upward and then glared at it. It was so wrong. Too stilted, too traditional, too like every other chapel that had ever been built. While he was at it, he shattered the lines of the freshly drawn walls with his pencil, too. With one last disgusted glance, he crumpled this latest effort at designing a chapel for La Torchere.

And then he stiffened. Someone was coming. He could hear light footsteps crunching up the rise toward where he sat. He had no wish to see anyone, to answer nosy questions, to reveal his sketches, to pretend he did not see the sidelong glances directed at the left side of his face.

Had he always been this antisocial? The short answer was no, but now he got a perverse sort of pleasure from his solitude. He resented intrusions into it. He looked about for a place to slip away. With his newfound eccentricities he was perfecting the art of being invisible.

But what if it was her?

What if it was Cynthia? Would she guess he was the man from last night? And how would she react if she did guess?

A reluctant smile tickled his lips. She probably had snootiness down to an art form by now. She'd had eight years since high school to work on it. When she recognized him as the man from last night—and a man from her past—she'd probably smack him across the face like some regally offended Southern belle.

A reaction he admitted he deserved.

And then he'd take her wrists in his hands and lean toward her and inhale the scent of her right before he…

"Mr. Barnett, there you are!"

Reality collided with fantasy. For it was not Cynthia who entered his small private world, but Merry Montrose. Lost in his thoughts of what-ifs he had lost his opportunity to escape. He regarded Ms. Montrose with resignation.

For a homely woman, he thought, she had the bearing of royalty. She was dressed beautifully, in a silk slack suit of the deepest shade of rose. She carried herself with an assurance and grace that belied the way she looked. She carried herself like a damned princess.

"Well," she said, pleased. "What a lovely surprise to find you here. Is this a spot you're thinking of for my chapel?"

"I haven't chosen a spot," he said, then sighed. "You've actually arrived just as I'm debating resigning the commission."

"It's perfect," she breathed, as if he had not said he was thinking of quitting. She looked around, her sharp gaze taking in all the details of the little clearing.

"I may be the wrong man for the job," he said, because she appeared not to have gotten the message the first time.

"Of course you aren't." She dismissed him with a wave of her hand. "Only the right man for the job could have found this place. I've walked here from time to time before and never realized its potential. Why, I can almost see the chapel right where you are sitting."

"It's good that one of us can visualize the chapel. I can't seem to come up with anything."

She stooped and picked up one of the discarded drawings, uncrumpled it, and studied it carefully. "This is nice."

He snorted. He was not sure there was a word he despised as much as *nice*—especially when it was used to describe his work. "Yeah. Nice. Ordinary. Uninspired."

"I'm sure you are just at the preliminary design stages. Am I correct?"

"The problem, Ms. Montrose—"

"Merry, please."

"—is that I need to understand the function of a building before I can design it."

"The function seems fairly simple to me," she said. "A wedding chapel is generally for weddings."

"And an office building is for offices, but there is always something underneath the function, more subtle, harder to grasp."

"You are more than an architect," she decided happily. "You are an artist."

He looked at her suspiciously. Had she peered in the window of his suite and seen the carving taking shape in there? A carving inspired by an encounter with a nymph from the sea?

"What do you think is *underneath* the function of the chapel, Mr. Barnett?"

"Rick," he corrected her, then contemplated her question. "Underneath the function of a wedding chapel run the things that I understand the least—trust, faith, love, hope."

"I don't believe that," she said firmly. She actually shook a finger at him as though he were a naughty boy.

"No disrespect to you, Merry, but it doesn't really matter what you believe," he said slowly. "I have to feel it, I have to understand those things somehow before I can design a building that glorifies them. Understand them? Merry, I'm not even sure I believe in them."

"Honestly, Mr. Barnett, I believe there is a romantic hiding under that cynical exterior."

He snorted. "I hardly think so."

She plucked another crumpled paper off the ground and

looked at it. "What's wrong with this one? It's beautiful. Oh, my. Better than anything I could have imagined. Why you rascal, lying to an old woman."

"Lying to you?"

"Only a romantic could design a chapel that looked like that."

She used her hand to smooth out the worst of the wrinkles and put the drawing in front of him. "Don't throw it out."

It was his least favorite from the work he'd done today. It reminded him of a chapel you might find at Disneyland, all soaring roof lines, castlelike turrets, and intricate gingerbread design details. It was gorgeous and glamorous and not quite real.

"Ah, yes," he said cynically. "The fairy tale. Hopes, dreams, happily ever after. All that kind of nonsense."

"You've captured those very things quite well for a man who doesn't believe in them." She reached out a knobbly finger and traced the soaring arch of the entryway to the chapel.

He pressed his own finger to the knot of tension he could feel growing on his forehead. "As I said, I'm not at all certain I'm the man for this job."

"And I'm more certain than ever that you are."

He snapped his book shut and got to his feet. "I won't make a decision about it today. It's getting too dark to do any more tonight, anyway."

"I hope you won't give up," she said gently, and he looked at her sharply. She seemed to be referring to much more than the chapel.

"Pardon?"

"Just give it a bit of time," she suggested. "You'll be amazed what comes to you."

"I suppose," he agreed, but with reluctance.

"What a lovely view of the beach," Merry said, changing the subject, wandering over to the edge of the small knoll they were on. "The sun's going down."

He joined her and watched the sun turn to fire then paint the ocean in ribbons of yellow and red and orange and gold before it dipped into the sea and was swallowed.

In one last fiery glow it illuminated a rock in the bay.

"Funny," he said, more to himself than to Merry, "I've never noticed that rock before. It looks astonishingly like a bear."

"Doesn't it?" she said, pleased for some reason. "You rather remind me of a bear yourself, Mr. Barnett."

"Wasn't I a closet romantic a moment ago? That's quite a leap," he said, and then realized, faintly astounded, he was teasing her.

"I'm sure there can be romantic bears," she said, her tone deliberately and dramatically doubtful.

He laughed, enjoying this strange woman for a reason he didn't quite understand. "Now you're being gracious," he said. "I probably reminded you of a bear because I'm crabby as hell."

She smiled. "And reclusive. And very, very powerful."

"I don't always feel powerful," he admitted. "Not anymore."

"A person's power is not in his appearance, Mr. Barnett. It is in the discovery of his spirit. Or hers."

He looked at her and realized she had probably been very beautiful once upon a time. She also looked as if she might be the type of woman who mourned the loss of her looks every day. And she had lost them naturally, to aging. She'd had time to get ready.

"If I take this diamond off my hand," she fluttered a ring the size of a golf ball in front of his face, "and rub it in the dirt, it doesn't change what it is."

What if half of it was shattered, like his face, he wanted to challenge her? Would that change what it was? Would that change its value?

But she looked like the type of woman, by turns annoying and amusing, who had an answer for everything, so he moved the subject away from the discomforting arena of what he had become since his accident. "It's interesting that I remind you of a bear. An old Native elder once honored me by telling me I had bear energy around me."

"Really?" she said, but somehow her tone of delighted surprise was feigned. It was as if she already knew. But how could she? That encounter had happened many years ago. Only two people had been present. As far as he could remember, he had never told anyone.

"It'll be totally dark in minutes," Rick said. He turned away from her to gather up his things—tape measures and sketchbooks, a camera, the discarded paper balls that littered the clearing. Night fell with incredible swiftness once the sun had done its spectacular swan dive into the sea.

"Oh, look, Rick, someone is coming to the beach. Odd, you'd think they would have arrived in time for the sunset."

He was at her side in a flash, but the person settling on the bench at the edge of the beach was not Cynthia.

"Oh, it's that poor young man. Baron Gunterburger."

Don't bite, he ordered himself. She obviously wanted to draw him into some delightful piece of gossip about the "poor" young man. A less poor-looking individual Rick could barely imagine.

The man carried himself with that faint standoffish arrogance of the very rich. He draped his arm possessively over the bench, regarded the sea. In the last of the light Rick could see the set of his face, the confidence in it.

Had he been that sure of himself once? Acted as though he owned the earth because he had a nice face, an athletic body, money, success?

He found himself disliking the man on principle. "What's so poor about him?"

"Sweet Wilhelm is used to getting his own way, especially with members of the fairer sex."

Another similarity between the man and his former self, Rick thought bitterly.

"And?"

"And he seems to have set his sights on a young lady who is not too interested in him. Unless she's changed her mind. Perhaps they are planning a romantic tryst on the beach. I do love a romantic tryst. Don't you?"

"No," he snapped grimly, but his mind was whirling.

A romantic tryst on the beach? This beach? But it was *his* beach! His and Cynthia's.

"In fact, it seems to me you said you knew the young lady in question."

He stared at Merry, dreading her next words.

"Didn't you say you'd been acquainted with Cynthia Forsythe at one time?"

He cursed soundly inside his own head. It took considerable strength to keep the word from coming out of his mouth. Cynthia was not meeting that man on *their* beach.

"Don't worry," Merry said and touched his arm. "She wasn't interested in him. They had breakfast together this morning, and there was no chemistry. Not on her part anyway."

How could she possibly know all that? And what would make her think he cared even if she did know?

"I wasn't worried," he said sharply, doing his best to hide the fact he was relieved that the Adonis down there had struck out over breakfast. Though how the hell would Merry Montrose be privy to that kind of information? If he asked, he would seem way too interested.

But then the second half of the equation registered with him.

Cynthia had had breakfast with another man?

When she'd been kissing him, Rick Barnett, last night? Not willingly, he reminded himself.

Ha. He'd take a bet on it: If that had not been a willing kiss he'd turn into a rock just like that one shaped like a bear.

Still, Cynthia had eaten breakfast with a baron. Rick could just guess Cyn's mama—good old Emma Bluebell or Bluebonnet, or whatever contrived thing she called herself—had been over the moon about that.

"Her mother seems to like him. The baron," Merry said.

"Her mother is here?"

"Yes. Cynthia works for her. A research assistant. They are holidaying together."

Cynthia, a research assistant? He remembered drawings she had done: sweeping lines and tantalizing colors. Where had that gone?

And she took holidays with her mother, that antagonistic old bat? What kind of life did the poor girl have, anyway?

"But Cynthia didn't like him? The baron?" He tried to act casually, inserting an I-couldn't-care-less note in his voice.

Merry shook her head gravely.

According to his source, who was standing watching him with quiet and observant interest, over the moon had not been Cynthia's reaction, thank God.

Still, one part of him said a baron was exactly what she deserved. She had made it clear, back in high school, that Rick was way out of his league, that she expected better things than what a boy from the wrong side of the tracks could ever give her. She hadn't worded it like that of course. No, it had all been so gentle and tasteful that there were even little diamond teardrops in her eyes.

He'd spent a good deal of his life proving her wrong. As he had conquered the world of architecture, other worlds, once closed to him, had opened. He dated women from those worlds, and with each conquest, he had thumbed his nose at the long ago Cynthia. He had become a success. Had he fantasized about meeting her one day to rub her nose in the fact that she had passed up a great guy?

Had he fantasized that she would get together with someone like the baron? Had he hoped she would live in some cold castle in Germany mending lederhosen and eating sauerkraut?

But this was not fantasy! This was reality, and part of him knew he had to stop her. She might come down to the beach to see him, Rick, and find that other guy there. What if she mistook him for the man who had kissed her last night? The baron looked just like the kind of arrogant ass who might think her arrival at the beach in the night was some kind of invitation.

Hadn't another arrogant ass arrived at the same conclusion last night?

It was different, he defended himself. She'd been swimming with not a stitch on. He'd had an old score to settle.

Not that it had worked. The score felt less settled than ever. In fact, Rick was left with the troubling thought that he had an obligation to rescue her from an unwanted "tryst" with the baron.

He had to stop her.

"There are other beaches for romantic trysts," Merry

said. "In fact, there is one on the other side of this bluff that is far more private."

"Really?" he said, trying not to appear too interested.

"I could have the concierge pack a basket. Chocolate, wine, strawberries, candles."

"That sounds like a great deal of trouble."

"Not at all. I love keeping the concierge busy. I could have her pack it and deliver it myself to protect your privacy."

He didn't feel that he had an ounce of privacy at the moment. This old woman seemed to know him—and his intentions—inside and out.

He could tell her she was crazy, that he had no one to share such a basket with, and walk away with his life intact. But what did he want his life intact for? What was he protecting? He might have known a moment ago, but right now he did not.

"All right," he said. "Go ahead and bring the basket to the beach. I don't mind paying you what it's worth."

He was not at all pleased with the self-satisfied smile that played across her face.

"Oh, no, Mr. Barnett, it's on the house. Please."

Merry watched him go, very satisfied indeed. She was getting better at this matchmaking stuff all the time. Too bad she would be giving it up soon.

Really, it was astounding how very little magic was required to bring two obviously well-suited human beings together. And it was a good thing that nature was fairly reliable, since her cell phone, such an interesting device in some of her former match-ups, was definitely now on the fritz. Last night she'd tried to get a glimpse of what was going on between Rick and Cynthia and had gotten a fascinating, but X-rated, look at a couple in a cabin in Canada.

Still, she could tell by the way both Rick and Cynthia were acting that it was in the works.

"Which means back to your gorgeous self soon," she sang to herself, accompanying the little tune with a twirl and a hug.

Perhaps magic was overrated. Sometimes all that was needed was an astute reading of human nature, planting a little seed strategically here or there, picking a book out of the trash, moving a bit of clothing from a closet to a bed…

Maybe putting the rock there hadn't even been necessary.

She gazed out at it, a rock that only three people in the world would ever see. Cynthia, Rick and herself.

How very interesting that a Native elder had once told him he had bear energy.

Perhaps the real magic was not anything she could manufacture. Perhaps real magic was already there, dancing in the air around people all the time, waiting for them to notice, to see. What were these marvelous coincidences that the universe provided so regularly and the average person overlooked just as regularly, if not magic? What was that thing that sparked in the air between a certain man and a woman, if not magic?

She hadn't done anything to make Cynthia and Rick, old sweethearts, arrive at the resort at the same time. And yet here they were, ready to rediscover each other.

And she was going to get the world's most fabulous chapel out of the deal as that man began the process of knowing his own heart.

"The world's a good place," she decided. And then smiled to herself. The old Merry would never have said that. Never noticed it. Not that her well-meaning, wicked godmother Lissa needed to know! Time to put Lissa the concierge to work. It delighted Merry to boss her godmother around. Mind you, Lissa would like getting that basket ready. Who knew? She might sprinkle in magic of her own.

"Back to your gorgeous self soon," Merry hummed in defiance of the deeper lessons she was learning. "And the rock is a very nice touch, if I do say so myself."

Cynthia glanced at the clock. It was only five minutes later than it had been the last time she looked. It was much too early to go to the beach.

It had been late last night when she had gone there. Midnight.

It was barely eight.

Would he be there?

What would it mean if he was?

She paced the suite restlessly, picked up *Hot Desert Kisses* and read just enough to make her groan. A well-meaning housekeeper seemed to have rescued the novel from the trash. Given the nearly new condition of the book, she must have thought it had been put in there by accident. She'd laid it carefully back on the reading desk.

Cynthia read just one page. The sheik was proud and fierce. But so was Jasmine. Still, Jasmine secretly loved the look of her captor's eyes, his lips…

Cynthia slammed the book back down. She didn't even know what her captor's eyes and lips looked like! What was she thinking? She didn't even have a captor. She had one kiss. She put the book on top of the fridge where she didn't have to look at it and then made the mistake of glancing once more at the clock.

Four hours until midnight! A woman could lose her mind in four hours.

She could not arrange her life on the flimsy excuse that

she might meet a man at midnight. An annoying man at that. One who was far too sure of himself and his devilish charm.

To hell with him, whoever he was. This was enough of living in a pins-and-needles world of waiting for something exciting to happen. She was in charge of her own life!

She would go dancing! Her mother would be thrilled. Wilhelm would be thrilled. She marched into her bedroom and slid to a halt.

There on the bed were the items she had purchased at the very swanky resort clothing store today. She blushed and glanced around. She could have sworn she put them away where her mother couldn't possibly see them. And where she couldn't see them herself.

What had possessed her to buy such things?

"Parris Hammond," she reminded herself.

Cynthia had met the newly engaged young woman at one of the resort's exclusive boutiques. Parris had been so full of life, sparkling with romance, so eager to spread around what she was feeling that she had enthusiastically pointed out outfits for both of them.

Cynthia edged closer to the bed, reached out and touched her new pajamas, which were lying there, right out in the open, beside her new bathing suit.

She was not even sure if the piece of film and lace she had purchased could be called pajamas.

More properly it was probably a negligee.

"Newlywed?" Parris had asked her with wicked delight, looking at her over a display of naughty underwear. "Men can't resist red, can they?"

Unnerved, since Cynthia had absolutely no idea what men could or couldn't resist, she had smiled in answer. A mistake, since Parris had then taken it as encouragement.

"Let me show you this bathing suit I just saw, if your guy likes red. I just know it's your size."

What was the point of telling her there wasn't a guy who belonged to her, as *your guy* would insinuate? Why not just play along and have fun for once in her life?

And so beside the red negligee on her bed was a red bathing suit. One piece but not a tank style. No, the back dipped amazingly low and so did the neckline. It was impractical. It would probably be nearly impossible to swim in, and it would leave the most outrageous lines if she sunbathed in it.

Still, she'd put it on in the privacy of a well-appointed changing room and stared at herself in the mirror. She was transformed. From a bookish author's assistant to a woman whose life held all kinds of possibilities.

Not the least of which was Hot Tropical Kisses.

Seeking out her mother and the baron and going dancing suddenly had the appeal of being at a pickled-egg eating contest. Cynthia slid out of her clothes and put the bathing suit on. She knotted the matching pareo around her waist and twirled experimentally in front of the mirror. Her mind was made up, and, before she lost her nerve, she slipped on her sandals, picked up her towel and went out the door.

She had not gone far down the path when the shrubs crinkled beside her, and she saw a shadow fall over the path. The hair on the back of her neck rose, and then she caught a whiff of a scent she recognized.

Wine-dipped cigars and aftershave.

"Keep walking," a voice said, low, as sensuous as the scrape of a rough palm over soft, soft skin. "Now, stop."

He was behind her. If she timed it just right, she could turn—

"Don't turn around."

She wanted to whoop for joy. Instead she said, coldly, "And who are you? A pervert, hanging around in shrubs and on deserted beaches, ready to jump out and demand kisses?"

"At least I'm fully clothed."

"How do I know that?"

He laughed, and it was a low rumble, every bit as sexy as his voice and his scent. "You'll have to take my word for it."

"I'm counting to three, and then I'm turning around."

"Don't," he said. "Please." The voice was practically in her ear, warm and sensuous and rough. His hands touched her shoulders, and she felt the hardness of the palms.

The humor was gone from his voice. He really didn't want her to see him. Why? Could a man who owned such a voice, such a body as she had glimpsed last night, be ugly? Would that be why he didn't want her to see him?

For some reason she did not want to let him know she had guessed that, perhaps because he might slip away and never come back.

And something in her heart ached foolishly at the thought of him never coming back.

"Humph," she said. "You still don't want me to get that description for the authorities."

"That's true," he said easily, "especially because of what I have planned for you tonight."

"Planned?" she asked, and ordered herself, sternly, *don't swoon. Cynthia, keep your head.*

On the other hand, she had kept her head her entire life and what had that gotten her? A boring existence where the closest thing she had to excitement was a girl named Jasmine who'd had the bloody good fortune to be kidnapped by a sheik.

"I'm going to kidnap you," he said in her ear.

Maybe it wasn't the housekeeper who had retrieved the book from the trash. "Have you been in my room?" she demanded.

"In your room?" he asked with genuine surprise. "What on earth have you got in your room that would make a man want to kidnap you?"

"Wouldn't you like to know," she said tartly.

"I would," he agreed. He slid a white strip of cloth around her head and over her eyes. He tied it with exquisite gentleness.

"What are you doing?"

"I already told you. Kidnapping you."

"I could scream," she told him.

"Mmm-hmm, you could."

"I could outrun you."

"No doubt."

"I could probably give you a black eye."

"I'm surprised you haven't."

"It would be insane to go along with this." That was her mother's voice, registering a token protest.

"Really? Why? We're on a well-populated island. There are people everywhere. There is only one way on and off, so I can't go very far with you against your will. What's so insane about saying yes to a small adventure, to saying yes to something you've never done before?"

"You don't know that I've never been kidnapped before," she told him.

"You don't have the look of a woman who has embraced adventure."

That silenced her. It cut to the quick. Even in her new bathing suit? She would show him she was exactly the kind of woman who embraced adventure.

Her mother would tell her to regard this whole incident with suspicion. Her mother, had she known what was taking place, would have been flapping around like a chicken who had just caught a whiff of a coyote inside the henhouse.

But she was not her mother.

It occurred to her now that she had sometimes trusted her mother's instincts above her own. Just like the young woman in the story she had heard today.

And look where that got her. Married to a rock.

"Well, pretty lady, what do you say?"

For once in her well-ordered life she was saying yes, but that's not what she said to him. To him she said, "If I had a say, it wouldn't very well be a kidnapping, would it?"

He chuckled and the sound made her world seem right. It was as if she knew him.

And then his hand found hers, and his arm went over her shoulder.

"Trust me," he whispered.

"You aren't supposed to trust kidnappers," she said, but leaned into him nonetheless, letting herself be guided down a path that she was pretty certain would lead to a brand-new way of looking at life.

Ready or not.

Chapter Four

"Where are we going?" Cynthia asked, even as she became aware that she didn't really care. She was with him. It felt as if that was all that mattered.

"I have a surprise for you."

A surprise for *her*. She felt pathetically eager, like a child who had never had a birthday party and was about to be given one.

Of course, it wouldn't do for him to know that!

"What if I don't like surprises?" she asked.

"You do," he said with supreme confidence, as if he knew her, as if he knew things about her that she did not know about herself.

"Humph," she said, but it seemed like a weak attempt at showing some spirit, but his solid form behind her, his hand on her elbow, guiding her through a dark world, drained the fight from her. She felt as if her bones were melting; the experience was compelling. *Erotic* would not have been too strong a word.

Though admittedly her experience in the erotic department was somewhat limited.

Make that nil.

A faint worry pierced her happiness, and she voiced it. "What if someone sees us?"

"Do you worry very much about what people think?"

"Yes!" Though it was less true now than it had been ten minutes ago. She was falling in love with his voice. It was so rough and low, raspy. His voice had the effect of a physical touch it was so powerful and distinctive. Apparently he did not care what people thought, and she contemplated how freeing that would be.

She had cut her eye teeth on the words, *Really, Cynthia, what would people think?*

"If anyone was to see us," he told her softly, "which is highly doubtful, they would probably only be charmed. A man enamored, leading a beautiful young woman to a surprise. They might smile and wonder whether we are lovers. Especially if I did this."

His lips touched the nakedness of her shoulder, lingered there. She gasped, despite herself.

"Well, I hope you don't think I'm charmed," she said, fighting the wild hammering of her heart. Fighting the feeling that she stood on the very edge of her control, and that she might fall—or leap—over that edge. In her heart she knew she was more than charmed. She was losing herself to him. She had to fight. "And you're not enamored. You don't even know me."

He sighed. "I think I should have put the scarf over your mouth instead of your eyes. Shh. Enjoy."

"Enjoy what?" she demanded, feeling her power slipping away from her, wanting to beg him to touch her shoulder with his lips again. "I'm being kidnapped by a lunatic."

"Sometimes when vision goes, other senses are heightened," he told her softly. "Can you feel that? Can you focus on what you are sensing now that you might have not ever noticed before?"

She had never noticed before that a man's lips on a woman's shoulder could turn her to putty, something completely pliable and waiting to be molded.

She was going to make a smart-aleck remark, something that hid the intensity of what she was experiencing rather than reveal it, but something stopped her.

She was suddenly aware that her captor was speaking from experience. Was he blind? Obviously not. But his vision might be impaired. A strange time to remember one of the facts she had learned about bears, but remember it she did.

Bears had extremely poor eyesight. They compensated. Their other senses were uncanny, especially their ability to smell and hear.

She felt herself surrender slightly more. The silk scarf tied around her eyes threw her into a world of blindness, and yet she was left with the exquisite sensation of every other sense being heightened. Even the silk pressed against her eyes—knotted on the back of her scalp, touching her cheeks—created a blissful sensation.

His scent and his touch became her world. He smelled of good things, real things, earth and soap, a clean masculine scent that was heady.

And his touch radiated unconscious strength, mastery.

She was blind and yet as she leaned into him and let him guide her down the path, she felt increasingly as though she could see for the very first time. She could see a world that held endless promise, a world of magic, a world where what was unseen was as important as what was seen.

She could feel the strength of his spirit, and again she was left with a sense of knowing who he was, totally, completely. Seeing him might only have distracted her.

Cynthia was aware that when you saw people you made judgments. They were too short or too tall or too thin or too heavy. Their noses were too sharp or their lips were too pursed. And all those judgments could keep a woman from experiencing what she was experiencing right now.

Hope.

Hope that perhaps a power called love really did exist after all. *Love?*

"Whoa," she said out loud, and inwardly she scolded herself, *way too fast, girl.*

And that described the beating of her heart, way too fast, as if she was standing on a cliff overlooking a deep and inviting tropical pond, trying to decide whether to jump.

He thought her uttered directive meant she had lost her footing and his grip on her tightened.

"All right?" he growled in her ear.

She could not say never better! Could she? No, it would reveal far too much about her pathetic life. So, she just leaned closer into his proffered strength, wondering when she had last allowed herself to lean. She loved independence. She loved being an independent woman. How could it possibly feel so good to allow another to take charge and lead?

"Where are you taking me?" she asked again, but this time she didn't mean just physically. What unexplored regions of her heart were about to be explored? Was she ready?

"I'm taking you to a place of such inky darkness that you cannot tell where the sea ends and the night begins, to a place where darkness blurs the lines between what is real and what is not."

Cynthia shivered. The words were eerily similar to the

ones Merry had used in creating the setting for the legend she had told her.

"What are we going to do there?" Cynthia asked.

He laughed softly, and his voice was a caress in her ear. "Swim. Eat. Talk. We are going to find the sun in total darkness."

"Ah," she said, and could not keep the bliss from her voice, "a poet kidnapper."

"Some women inspire poetry," he said.

She actually tripped in surprise, then felt his arm steadying her. "And I'm not one of them!"

"Whatever gave you such a ridiculous idea?" he said gruffly, with disapproval. His voice was low and throaty, and even though she could not see him, those heightened senses told her exactly what was going to happen next.

He stopped, and she felt him move to stand in front of her. His fingers rested lightly on the nakedness of her shoulders, and then one hand moved to touch the bottom of her chin and lift it up.

She could feel him studying her intently. She sensed his appreciation and wanted desperately to study him in return.

But before the urge became too powerful to resist and she pulled the white silk mask away from her eyes, his lips touched hers.

Not as they had last night. Not with domination, not as part of a wicked game, but gently, in greeting, in welcome.

"Oh, God," she managed to whisper against the softness of his lips, before she gave herself over to him and to all he promised. Her lips parted under the gentle pressure of his. She felt the steely strength in his arms as he gathered her close. She was stunned by the sensation of touching him so intimately, her body quivering against the length of his. For the first time, she felt the physical power of him and realized she had underestimated it. She felt it all—the broad, hard planes of his chest, the flatness of his belly, the powerful leanness of his legs.

She could have pulled away, and perhaps she should have pulled away, but she didn't. She pressed herself closer to him, greedy for his warmth and power, captivated completely by the searing energy of him.

His kiss deepened as she pushed closer. Far-off waves suddenly seemed to be crashing inside her own head. He tasted of rain and truth and the earth and secrets deep and lovely.

He had been absolutely right. The sun was coming out in her darkness.

And then, abruptly, with no warning, he lifted his lips from hers. She heard the tiniest mew of protest leave her own lips as they experienced the terrible sense of loss.

Muscles that had been relaxed, tensed. He was like an animal, alert to dangers she could not begin to sense. But she guessed he was listening, hearing something that she didn't hear.

"What?" she asked. She curled her arm around his neck, trying shamelessly to pull him back to her. But he disengaged her, and the contact between them was lost.

She sensed him move away from her, silent as the night, and then he stepped back behind her one last time.

He kissed the back of her neck, his lips warm, his breath hot. The tingle went down to her toes.

Then the blindfold slid from her eyes and for a moment she was stunned by the stillness and the silence of the dark, dark night.

And then she realized he was gone.

She frowned, standing there, not knowing what to do or even where she was exactly. And then she heard what he must have heard already. Female laughter, a man's low voice, a low whirring sound that she couldn't quite place.

And then a golf cart came careening around a curve in the path.

Cynthia had to leap to get out of the way. She caught a glimpse of a woman on the passenger side and felt the shock of recognition. It was her mother, but not her mother—a woman of abandon, wild and windblown, laughter-filled. Jerome Carrington, with none of his customary dignity, was at the helm of the speeding golf cart, making loud engine noises. He was apparently pretending he was driving the Indy instead of a nearly silent cart on a deserted pathway.

In that moment as they whirred by her, Cynthia registered, with shock and disbelief, her mother's look of reckless abandon.

Was there something about this place then—about La Torchere—some magic in the air that made people something they had not been before? Made them embrace parts of themselves previously disowned?

She thought of the disintegration of her own control, and suddenly a doubt inserted itself in her. How good a thing was it to lose control?

Her mother had warned her all her life about these kinds of mistakes, and where they could land a woman. Barefoot and pregnant in the trailer court, an undershirt-clad husband swilling beer and watching football in the next room.

Jerome and Emma had passed and Cynthia sighed with relief, thinking she had been granted a momentary reprieve. But then she heard her mother's voice.

"Stop! Jerome, that was Cynthia."

Before Cynthia could disappear as surely as her mystery man had, the golf cart was backing up. It stopped beside her.

She was not sure who was regarding who with more surprise.

"What are you doing?"

They both asked the question at precisely the same time.

"Jerome is taking me on a tour of the whole island," her mother said.

"At high speed, in the dark," Cynthia pointed out, hoping to get the upper hand fast and first. "You nearly ran me down. Why, it was reckless!"

"I apologize," Jerome said with gallant sheepishness. "Your mother makes me feel young and foolish again."

Her mother batted her eyelashes coquettishly in his direction before favoring Cynthia with a much different look.

"Well, we weren't expecting to see anyone out wandering the paths in complete darkness." Her eyes narrowed. "Where are you going?"

"Just for a swim."

"But the pool isn't this way."

"Um, I wasn't exactly going to the pool."

"You were going to a beach? You were going to swim in the ocean? In the dark? Cynthia, no!"

Such horror should have been reserved for a more dramatic adventure—bungee-jumping naked before a packed press gallery—but her mother had never been one to reserve horror.

"Bluebird, why not?" Jerome asked. "It's a gorgeous night. I might have suggested a swim in the sea myself, had I thought of it."

If he had, Cynthia thought cynically, he would have found himself swimming by himself. Her mother did not swim. She did not like what water did to her carefully coiffed hair, not to mention her makeup.

"Why not?" Emma said indignantly, rounding on Jerome. "Why not? Swimming alone is dangerous. What if a shark attacked her? And there are all kinds of sharks, most of them not inhabitants of the ocean! Maybe she wouldn't have even made it to the beach. She's a woman alone out here. Dressed like that. My God!"

"It's not exactly the high-crime zone of East L.A.," Jerome pointed out, and then looked at Cynthia. "Dressed like what?"

"Get in the cart, Cynthia," her mother said through tight lips, not even deigning to answer Jerome's innocent question.

But Cynthia knew. Her mother thought her new bathing suit was unsuitable. Trashy, just like her reading material.

It occurred to Cynthia that only moments ago she had convinced herself of what an independent young woman she was.

But now she could see that it was a lie. Her whole life felt, sadly, like a lie, as if she had lived it for someone else other than herself. She had never been reckless. She had never been out of control, and she had always considered those good things. Now, she wasn't sure.

"Get in the cart," her mother said again, her voice taking on a familiar shrill edge.

Cynthia could see quite a scene unfolding if she didn't do as her mother asked. Her mystery man must still be lurking in the shrubs somewhere, and she didn't want him to witness such a thing.

And poor Jerome needed to be spared, too, though why she would not want him to have a complete picture of her mother's rather ferocious temper was beyond her.

But there was more to her complying with her mother's wishes. Tonight, Cynthia had come face to face with another side of herself.

It frightened her.

Just as it had frightened her once, a long, long time ago when she had ridden on the back of a speeding motorbike. That boy, too, had had a gift for bringing out her wild side, for bringing her to the edge of her self-control. It had scared the heck out of her then, and it did now, too.

Jerome cast her a sympathetic look as she got in the back of the cart. The ride to their rooms was done considerably more slowly than the speed Jerome and her mother had been traveling at under their own steam. And much more silently.

She could tell by the set of her mother's shoulders that she was bristling, barely containing her bad temper for Jerome's sake.

They dropped Cynthia at her suite.

"I'll just say good night to Jerome and be right in to talk to you," her mother said, as if Cynthia was a wayward teenager who had been caught with the smell of booze on her breath at the senior high prom.

Her head held high, Cynthia marched into her room and shut the door.

She got the impression Jerome was none too happy with her mother. Their voices carried through her open windows, her mother's becoming more and more shrill while his became lower and calmer.

Moments later the knock came on the adjoining door. Emma didn't even wait for Cynthia to answer it. She let herself in and stood there, her arms folded, her foot tapping, her gaze stripping Cynthia bare.

"Tell me what on earth is going on." It was an order, not a request.

Cynthia felt her chin tilt up stubbornly. "I told you. I was going swimming."

"You do not go swimming alone at night! Good grief.

As if swimming alone isn't an obvious enough hazard, what if a man with bad intentions saw you in that getup!"

"Getup?" Cynthia asked icily.

"That is not the type of suit a well-bred young woman parades around in. I am shocked at you." She sighed and shook her finger at Cynthia's mutinous expression. "Sometimes blood shows, I'm afraid."

"What does that mean?" Cynthia asked, slowly, carefully, furiously.

"It means sometimes I see your father in you, and it frightens me."

Cynthia felt as though she had been slapped, and she drew herself to her full height, several inches taller than her diminutive mother. "You know, mother, you missed everything that was best about that man. You missed his spontaneity and his boldness and his love of adventure. I hope I have kept some of those qualities alive. I hope I have. I hope it isn't too late."

"You've met a man," her mother deduced after a scorching silence. "I knew it when I saw you this morning with that glazed look on your face. And I bet he's an absolute scoundrel, isn't he? Why else would you be too ashamed of him to introduce me?"

"Mother," Cynthia said, measuring every word, "I work for you, which I am just beginning to realize may be a mistake. Did you know I once dreamed of being an artist?"

"An artist? Oh, starving to death in a garret is such charming fun!"

Cynthia could see there was no point in arguing, so she said very carefully, "I am twenty-six years old, and if I want to swim at night—in the buff—"

"In the buff?" her mother squeaked with horror.

"I am going to. And if I want to see a man, I am not

going to ask your permission. I am going to have my own life, and if you can't accept that, then—"

"Then what?" her mother whispered, and tears pooled in the blueness of her eyes.

Cynthia remembered her promise. She'd look after her. She'd make her happy.

But at what price? The price of her own happiness?

"Cynthia," her mother said, her tone entirely changed, that of a small girl, "don't be mad. I'm your mother. I just want what's best for you."

"I need to be alone," Cynthia said, but more gently. "Could you just leave me alone?"

Her mother touched her temple and winced.

I feel a migraine coming on, Cynthia thought silently.

"I feel a migraine coming on," her mother said.

"How convenient for you," Cynthia said before she could stop herself.

"That's exactly the kind of thing your father used to say to me." Her mother gave a cry of pure pain, before she turned and ran out the door.

Cynthia felt a deep exhaustion settle over her. She should go and soothe her mother, but she was sure part of the cause of her exhaustion was all the *shoulds* that ruled her life, not to mention having allowed herself to be manipulated for so long.

On the other hand, she could go back out and try to find her mystery man, but she no longer felt like it.

Her mother was probably right. She was dancing with danger. She was making foolish, irresponsible decisions. Emotion was ruling her rather than reason.

Control was a good thing, and how could she have remained in control tonight? She had barely maintained her control when he had kissed her shoulder. And then her lips. What kind of danger would the rest have brought? Swimming, talking, eating together?

She took off her bathing suit, reluctantly. She stared at the red negligee but her defiance was all used up for one night. She didn't even feel like the same woman who had purchased it. Instead, she shoved the bathing suit and negligee in a bag and put them under the bed. She donned the old bunny pajamas. *Hot Desert Kisses* was on the night table.

She crawled into bed and read one paragraph. Jasmine and her sheik were kissing with an unbridled passion that made Cynthia feel hollow. She threw the book at the wall, laid her head on her pillow and wept.

Not so much because of the argument with her mother, either, but because of the opportunity missed.

Where had he planned to take her tonight? He had said they were going to swim together in darkness.

The picture was so compelling and so erotic that she cried harder for having missed it.

What if he thought she'd chosen her mother over him, and what if he never came back?

It occurred to her she was pining for a complete stranger. She didn't even know his name.

Rick waited until they had gone and the night once again belonged to him. He followed the cart until he saw it stop and saw which unit Cynthia went into. He left when her mother's shrill voice began to pierce the blessed quiet of the night. He crossed to the secluded beach he had chosen for his "tryst" with Cynthia.

He kicked sand over the candles that burned around the blanket and the midnight lunch he'd had delivered by a very willing Merry. He was hardly able to appreciate the romantic setting she had created for them. He rolled up the blanket, stuffed it on top of the basket, and stripped off all his clothes.

He went into the dark water and tried to swim himself to exhaustion, to a place where he would not think about what it would be like to have shared this with her. He never did quite reach that place. Frustrated, he packed his ruined evening under his arm and returned to his suite.

It was over then. It was no different from last time.

Only Cynthia was now a full-grown woman and still under her mother's thumb. How willingly she had climbed into that golf cart, like a chastised child. He tried not to think of the look of abject distress on her lovely features as she had looked back over her shoulder into the darkness, searching for him.

He rarely slept at night anymore. He had adopted it as the time when his scars showed the least, and there was the least opportunity to run into people, well-meaning, curious, and cruel by turns.

The night was his. It belonged to him. And yet tonight he felt weary almost beyond reason. That very weariness made him vulnerable. Vulnerable to the way she had looked tonight with her bathing suit so sensual, the erotic sweep of the filmy wrap around her legs, the sexy red against the creaminess of her skin, the plunging line at the back showing off her every curve.

He thought of the energy that had pulsed around them. She had not been afraid of him. At the first sign of fear he would have called the game off.

No, she had been spunky and wide open to whatever adventure he was planning. Her lips, under his, had been hungry, passionate, promising.

Should he try again?

No. Even tonight, he had lied to her. He had known if

people came upon them he would disappear, because he had known they would not look at them, at him and Cynthia, and see enamored young lovers.

No, they would see her face. And his. Beauty and the Beast.

It worked in fairy tales. But in real life? He reached for his sketchpad, pondering whether or not he should try again. Why? Where was it all going? Even if she had matured to a point where she would choose him, and not her mother, *why* would she choose him?

He went to the mirror and looked, to savagely remind himself what he now was.

Half of his face remained what it had always been. He remembered that boy. His careless good looks, the perfection of his smile, how he had used it so wickedly to get his own way.

Cynthia was beautiful. She could have any man in the world, including Baron Gruntermunger or whatever his name was.

"Leave her to her life," he commanded himself. "And get on with yours."

His life. His work.

He went to the table which he had set up as a desk, and opened his sketchbook. Stuck in it was the drawing of the chapel that Merry had retrieved from the ground. She had liked it, but he looked at it critically.

He knew suddenly exactly what he didn't like about it. It was that it didn't tell the whole story. The chapel was too perfect and too beautiful, something out of a fairy tale. But there were hard places people traveled to, long before they ever made it to the church. They had to find their way through unmapped territory, over mountains, they had to face the barren places in their own souls.

He found himself drawing low, sweeping stairs. He would make them of unbroken slabs of black granite. They would represent the climb, the cold places, the challenging uphill parts of falling in love. And the floor of the church, too, in the same black granite, to represent the hard times and hard decisions. People who found themselves walking up the aisles of churches committing to something for the rest of their lives had experienced a great deal more than the pure bliss his one drawing had captured. No, there was torment mingled with the happiness, of that he was certain.

He stared at the drawing. He was acting as if he was going to build that chapel after all.

Worse, he was acting as though he knew something of the subject of love.

"Ha," he said. "I've designed a set of stairs and a floor." That was a long, long way from designing an entire building.

And still when he looked at it, he knew he was moving in the right direction.

And with Cynthia? Was he moving in the right direction with her?

He thought he had decided that. He was accustomed to being a man of decision. Why was he revisiting this? It was over. Before it started, it was over, which was good. No one was hurt yet.

Not her by him revealing what he looked like. Not him by her rejection of that.

He put away his sketchbook and got up restlessly.

On the low coffee table beside his couch was a carving he had begun, and nearly half finished, the night before. He frowned. He was almost positive he had put the carving away in the drawer of his nightstand beside the bed. The image emerging from the wood troubled and delighted him.

This artistic part of himself was something he had always kept hidden. He had noticed it emerging tonight, something almost poetic in the way he'd spoken to Cynthia.

That was the good part of anonymity. It allowed him to be totally himself, even to experiment a bit with what that meant.

Rick Barnett, serious and successful architect, could not have whispered poetic words to Cynthia about what he had planned for them. He could not have said they were going to swim in darkness until they found the sun. No, that man had to keep his macho image firmly in place, never show a sensitive side, which he had always perceived as weakness.

Now, turning the partly finished carving over in his hands, he was not so sure what was weakness and what was strength.

Rick carved with wood that he found. Though there were certain softer woods that lent themselves to this art, he much preferred to be out for a walk and come across some treasure—a chunk of beautifully grayed driftwood, a stump of oak. He loved how wood seemed so hard and implacable but in actual fact moved like a lover beneath the carver's hands. The more experienced the carver became in the medium, the more the piece of wood gave up its secrets, allowed itself to be shaped, gave itself completely to design.

The figure he was working on was very small, less than six inches high. The wood was a piece of driftwood, a particularly dark piece, with light sections swirling through it. It lent itself perfectly to the concept of a woman in the night, but it was laced with light as if the moon touched her. His carving depicted a woman emerging from the water, her hands lifted above her head.

He had captured an amazing amount of emotion in the

simple lines of the carving. The woman was saying a joyous yes to the embrace of life and freedom.

He picked it up now and allowed himself to be seduced by it, pulled into it. With a sigh, he got out his tools and worked on it ceaselessly. An hour before dawn, it was done.

He realized, suddenly, it did not belong to him. It belonged to Cynthia. He would leave it for her then, a farewell gift. He had never given away a carving before. He had always felt compelled to keep this secret part of himself private, away from judgments.

How could he be so certain she would not judge him? Because once she had been an artist herself? Because of the way her lips had opened underneath his like a flower absorbing rain?

He went, cloaked in night, down the path to the unit where he had seen the golf cart drop Cynthia off.

It was a ground-floor suite, probably identical to his own.

He stood there in the darkness. One of the French doors off her patio was open. If he'd had any doubts about her "kidnapping" scaring her, they left him now. She was obviously not afraid. And if the design was the same as his unit, that door led right to her bedroom.

He imagined the sound of her sleeping, her breath quiet and gentle, like a purr. He imagined the way she would look, the honey of her hair spread across the pillow, her brow damp with the humidity in the Florida air. He imagined her cheeks would be flushed with sleep and heat, and he hoped she was dreaming of kisses.

Standing there in the darkness, the whole world asleep, Rick allowed himself to feel what he had not allowed himself to acknowledge ever since a wall on a building project had collapsed on top of him and changed his life forever.

He felt lonely beyond words.

And he felt the hopelessness of trying to change that.

Quietly, he moved through darkness. The night was leaving, becoming ever so faintly tinged with the dawning light of a new day. He put the carving on the table on her patio and resisted the temptation to look in on her.

Still, as he turned to leave, the growing light disoriented him. When night melted into day and the shadows changed and intensified, he stumbled over one of the deck chairs. It was made of metal and it crashed against the glass top of her patio table with a terrible clang before it fell to the ground with a resounding clatter that seemed to echo endlessly through the sleeping resort.

He backed hastily into the flowering shrubs. The carving was undisturbed on the table. He held his breath, waiting.

And then he let it out. Nothing. No movement. No lights coming on in her unit or in any of the neighboring ones. He had just turned to leave when a movement caught his eye.

Cynthia emerged from the room and onto the patio. She looked adorable, her hair scattered, her eyes faintly puffy, the mark of the sheet where her cheek had pressed her pillow tattooed the perfection of her skin.

Even though her pajamas looked like something a child would wear, longing washed over him. But he leveled all his steely strength against it.

She looked about sleepily, stretched, looked toward the line of pink growing in the eastern sky. Then she saw the gift that had been left on her table.

The sleep left her face and was replaced with absolute delight as she reached for it. She studied it, her face lit in the first strong rays of morning sun. She ran her fingers with gentle reverence over the smoothness of the grayed wood. And then, in that moment when she was so sure she was alone, she pressed the figure against her lips. She embraced her gift to her bosom and scanned the walkway in front of her suite. She stepped off the ground-level patio stones and looked both ways down the deserted walkways.

He recognized her longing as equal to his.

But she could fill his with her beauty alone. How could he ever fill hers?

Still, his strength dissolved. He watched as she turned, gave one last look over her shoulder and went back inside.

She did not lock the door behind her.

"Tonight, sweet lady," he said, and felt the exquisite bliss and torment of that decision.

Chapter Five

She had gone back to sleep, but when she opened her eyes again, the first thing Cynthia saw was the carving. She smiled and stretched, feeling how sweet and untroubled her sleep had been, almost as if the gift had watched over her and blessed her. Now she sat up in bed and looked at the carving again. It was simple, and yet it had captured so much—a young woman reaching for life, for freedom.

Was the young woman her? And what did it mean that she had found this small gift? Was it even from her mystery man?

"I think I'll call him M&M, short for Mystery Man," she said out loud. When she picked up the carving she had no doubt it was from him. It was as if she could feel his spirit carved into the sensuous curve of the wood, as if part of him remained.

What was more perplexing was the question of whether or not the gift was tied to the legend of the bear. It was preposterous to entertain such an imaginative thought. Part of what made her a great research assistant was her ability to think logically, to organize information in ways that made sense.

It made no sense to think that a bear leaving gifts for a woman in a story would lead to strange parallels in her own life. It made no sense to think that way, but that's the way she was thinking.

A knock came on her door, firm and masculine.

Her breath caught in her chest. Only one man, that she could think of, would be knocking on her door with such no-nonsense authority.

She threw on her housecoat and raced to the door, prepared to pull him inside, look him over, touch his face, *see* it, before she covered him with sweet kisses—

"Jerome!" she said with surprise after yanking open the door. She had to put on the brakes to keep herself from falling into his arms on the sheer forward momentum and enthusiasm that had carried her to the door.

"Good morning, Cynthia. I'm sorry. Were you expecting someone else?"

Yes, she wanted to wail. Instead she composed herself. "No, of course not. Who else would there be to expect?"

He looked at her quizzically, and she realized how she must look. Her cheeks flushed, her eyes heated, telegraphing her *wanting* him to be someone else. Embarrassed, she tugged her housecoat tighter around her and fastened the belt.

"I was supposed to have breakfast with your mother. She's not answering her door. I thought you might know if she's left already, or if she's not well."

"Migraine," Cynthia said with a sigh.

Jerome's eyebrow arched upward. "Migraine? Does she get one of those every time she tries to manipulate someone?"

Cynthia stared at him. Why, it seemed as if Jerome Carrington had her mother's number after a very short period of acquaintance. Despite herself she chortled with appreciation.

He smiled, too. "Could I come in for a moment? There's something I would like to discuss with you."

Cynthia liked Jerome. Her mother had a tendency to pick men she could dominate, but Jerome was different. Strong. Way too sure of himself ever to allow anyone to push him around.

Her coffeemaker had come on automatically and the rich aroma of fresh brew filled her apartment. "Come have coffee," she invited.

She and Jerome sat down at her table and she poured him a cup. Sunshine splashed across the table, promising another beautiful day. Outside the window, palm trees swayed on gentle breezes, and flowers bloomed in breathtaking and exotic tropical abundance. Despite her initial disappointment that Jerome was not who she had hoped he would be, Cynthia felt herself looking forward to the day.

And then she asked herself when had been the last time she'd actually looked forward to a day?

"I'm going to ask you a personal question, Cynthia," Jerome said, "and I hope you won't think I'm being too terribly nosy."

"I don't see nosiness as part of your nature," she said.

"You might now." He hesitated, took a sip of his coffee and then asked, "Why do you allow your mother to behave the way she does with you?"

"And what way is that?" Cynthia hedged, but it seemed some of the pleasure she had been feeling in simple things, sunshine and the aroma of coffee, had evaporated.

"She's very bossy and domineering. She controls you."

Cynthia blew on her coffee and felt the complications of

her relationship with her mother drag her down as if she had been dropped in the ocean with an anchor attached to her ankle. But then she met Jerome's eyes. He offered her rescue, a safe harbor, someone she could trust with a secret.

She had never told anyone before about her promise to her father. She had carried it within her like a binding personal burden. She blurted it out now, with the relief of a devotee in confessional.

"So, if I understand you," Jerome said slowly, when she was finished, "on his deathbed, your father extracted a promise from you to make your mother happy."

She nodded. She was surprised to find she was crying, the tears slithering silently down her cheeks and plopping into her coffee.

"And how old were you?" Jerome asked gently.

"Sixteen," she choked.

Jerome smiled at her with such compassion that she had a sudden irrational wish that he was her father. His hand covered hers.

"Cynthia, I am sixty-eight years old, and that has one advantage over youth. I've learned a thing or two, so I hope you will allow me to share some of what I have learned with you, without being offended.

"The way I see this situation, you were a child trying to make the world right. I think this is a truth you probably know by now—people do not make each other happy. No person can be responsible for another person's happiness. Each person has a responsibility—I would go so far as to say a sacred one—to find their own happiness in this world.

"And I believe your father is in a place now where he would understand that simplest of truths, where he would release you from a burden he probably placed on you unintentionally. He was probably sick and in pain and on drugs. If he had thought through what he was asking of you, I don't think he would have asked it. I really don't."

Cynthia was crying openly, as relieved as if she was a prisoner who had suddenly been given the keys to freedom. She had only to find the right door, the right lock, and she was pretty sure she knew where that was.

"I have sensed in you from the beginning a truly adventurous spirit," Jerome said. "This passive face you show to the world is a complete masquerade. You have an artist's soul. I sense it. You are not doing your mother or yourself any favors by robbing the world of who you really are."

Cynthia dried her tears with a tissue and gave Jerome a watery smile. There were really no words big enough to express the gratitude she felt to him, but she tried anyway. "Thank you."

"Ah, you are welcome, my dear. Now go do something wild and crazy with your day. Be young."

"Drive a golf cart too fast?" she suggested mischievously.

"Oh, you can do better than that. I'm sure of it."

She laughed, and the laughter felt rich and good and real. "I believe I can."

"Now, is there a connecting door to your mother's room?"

Cynthia nodded toward it.

Jerome winked, got up and went through it. He left it ajar, and she heard him go into her mother's bedroom, and she heard her mother's loud squeak of outrage.

"Do you think I've never seen a woman without makeup before? Or without her hair done? I haven't led that sheltered a life, nor have you. Quit being ridiculous."

She couldn't quite hear what her mother said next, but her tone came through loud and clear—outraged, snobby, cutting.

But she certainly heard what Jerome said.

"Migraine, my ass!"

Cynthia had to bite her fist to keep a shout of laughter from coming out. She eavesdropped shamelessly.

"You can't get a migraine every time you don't get your own way. Your poor, sweet daughter has been spending the precious hours of her life trying to make you happy. Bluebird, you should be absolutely ashamed of yourself. Now, get up and get into that shower, or I'll put you in there myself."

Cynthia's eyes went very wide at that. No one ordered her mother around. She braced herself, waiting for the sounds of breakage—lamps shattering, phones hitting the wall—whatever was within reach would be in danger.

Instead, she was shocked to hear complete silence, and then the far-off sound of a shower turning on.

Good grief! Her mother had listened to someone? Surely if Jerome had followed through on his threat to put her mother in the shower himself there would have been enough shrieking to bring down even the well-constructed roof of their suites.

Another thought hit Cynthia, when all she could hear was the shower. Was her mother in it alone? She didn't want to know. She got up, tiptoed over to the connecting door, and pulled it shut.

Jerome had said she, Cynthia Forsythe, had a wildly adventurous spirit? That he saw an artist's soul? That seemed so unlikely! But on the other hand, when had she become so passive? Waiting for life to happen to her? Waiting for others to take control?

What had happened to that girl who had thought her life would be spent creating beauty? Either creating art herself, or having a small gallery where she displayed the work of others? What had become of those dreams? When had she become a sleepwalker in her own life, going where the current led her, instead of making her own waves?

For some reason the legend Merry Montrose had shared with her entered her mind again. It was as if her life was intertwined now with that story, whether she wanted it to be or not.

What had the young wife's role been? Why had she been so passive while her mother and her husband played such major roles? If you couldn't have the starring role in your very own life, who could?

"It's my turn," Cynthia decided, out loud, and liked the firmness in her voice, the absolute conviction of it. It was her turn and her time to live. And M&M had better watch out.

Cynthia got up and got dressed, aware of how unhappy she was with her limited choices. Knee-length pleated shorts. Cotton blouses in pastel colors. She looked through her wardrobe with a critical eye. Not a single thing in it would do. Not one thing was something she had picked because she'd liked it. It had all met her mother's approval. Cynthia's wardrobe was expensive, tasteful, classical and dull, dull, dull.

Did anything in her closet speak of an artist's soul or an adventurous heart? She wanted color instead of neutrals. She wanted boldness instead of conservatism. She wanted flow rather than rigidity. And she could start with her wardrobe!

An hour later, she tucked her credit card into the pocket of knee-length, knife-creased shorts that she was wearing for the very last time and headed out the door to the wonderful little mall at La Torchere. She hoped Parris would be there!

Merry Montrose stared at her cell phone, aghast. It was at her feet and it was in tiny pieces.

She really shouldn't have lost her temper and jumped up and down on top of it. Magic cell phones were hard to procure and difficult to replace.

"My girl," she said to herself, "your temper has always been a teeny problem in your life."

Still, a little temper was understandable. After she had set up that lovely romantic evening for Cynthia and Rick—that little beach hardly anyone knew about, candles in the sand, a blanket, a basket filled with champagne and chocolate—she hadn't even been able to check in and see how they were progressing.

It made her so mad she gave the destroyed phone one more little kick.

Well, there was nothing else to do about it except what ordinary people did when they wanted to see how their meddling had worked out. She'd have to ask. Cynthia or Rick? Cynthia was the more approachable of the two. She could probably milk all kinds of information out of her without the poor dear even knowing she was being milked.

But when she picked up her regular phone and dialed Cynthia's room, there was no answer. When she dialed Rick's, there was.

A harsh voice growled, "I'm not home," and the receiver was slammed down in her ear.

Which meant he was home. But his mood! Did that bode well for romance? It did not! Merry now felt frantic for the details of Rick and Cynthia's liaison last night.

Of course, she couldn't just waltz over there without an excuse. She'd have to pretend she had business about the new chapel. What, though? The resort owner was pressing her for a location? A price? She had to be careful. Rick had been a hair away from deserting the project last night. How about, she thought, if a signature was missing from the contract?

That would do nicely! She retrieved the contract. With her legal background it would be simple to insert a line. But it was even simpler just to wiggle her finger. She inserted a line on it that hadn't been there before.

"That's how magic is supposed to work," she told the cell phone as she stepped over it and headed across the resort to Rick's complex.

She found his place easily, and it was obvious he wasn't receiving guests. Possibly he was not even out of bed, which might explain the cantankerous tone of voice he had used on the phone. The complimentary morning paper was still on his step. All the curtains were drawn. The Do Not Disturb sign glared from his door handle.

"A shame," she said, "on a bright sunny day like this to be holed up inside a cave."

Then she giggled, because of course that is what bears did. They holed up inside caves on nice, sunny days.

It probably meant, she decided with a little shiver of delight, that his evening had gone exceptionally well. He had probably wooed that lucky Cynthia deep into the night. He was tired. He had slept in. Perfectly understandable.

She just couldn't wait to hear about it. She knocked on the door, dismissing the Do Not Disturb sign. It was obviously intended for housekeeping, not for her.

Then she heard a deep growl from within and felt a little quiver of doubt. It was probably not a good idea to disturb the bear within his den, but then Rick wasn't really a bear. What was he going to do, tear her head off?

She knocked again, though a little more timidly than was her nature.

He yanked open the door and she took a step back, wondering if her head was indeed in danger of being torn off.

Rick looked magnificent, in drawstring sweats and nothing else. The man was magnificently made, all rippling muscle and bronzed skin. But his expression was brooding, the scars on his face standing out harshly in the bright sun. His eye patch made him look exceedingly dangerous and his good eye flashed with irritation.

"What?" he snarled, not even a pretense of civilized politeness.

"I—I was just in the area and thought I'd drop off this contract. I noticed yesterday that you forgot to sign it in one place."

He took the contract from her with enough force to rip it in two. He didn't even glance at it. He stepped back from the door, and it was obvious he planned to shut it in her face!

"Er-hmm! Mr. Barnett?" She was pleased that she could still muster a royal tone when need be.

The door reopened marginally. "What?" he growled.

"I just wondered about last night. Um, you know, how it went."

He glared at her ferociously, then shut the door. A moment later, the door swung open. Out of the darkness the picnic basket she had packed so lovingly the night before was hurled at her. It landed with a thud at her feet.

"It didn't," he said, and slammed the door.

Merry looked down at the basket, back to the door, and back to the basket. "Oh, dear," she said. "This is very, very bad."

She scooped up the basket and walked away, somewhat dazed. She saw a bench beside one of the walkways and collapsed on it. Disconsolately, she sorted through the contents. The champagne was untouched; not a strawberry or chocolate was missing.

She felt as though she was going to weep. Not just for

Cynthia and Rick, but for herself. What if she was doomed to live like this forever? What if they didn't fall in love? Didn't even come close? What then?

She looked down at the wrinkles on her hands, the skin stretched paper-thin over bones and tendons, the knobbiness of her wrists.

"Everything all right, Ms. Montrose?"

It was that darned handyman. Every time she saw him, her heart did a little tumble. Or at least the heart of the younger woman who resided inside her tumbled.

He was gorgeous. All burnished muscle and astounding good looks. She had always liked blondes, especially in tropical climates. Their skin turned to brushed gold. His eyes were so intensely blue, riveting. If she were her normal self, he was just the kind of man she might have flirted with.

Or maybe not. She was a princess, after all. And he was a lowly laborer.

Although something about being old and ugly, and living the life of an ordinary working person, was making the kinds of judgments she had always made seem hopelessly outdated, not to mention horribly snobby.

It occurred to her, and not happily, either, that even if she was returned to her normal self, she was never going to be the same person she had been before.

With a little cry of dismay she leapt up from the bench and hurried away from the quizzical look of a gorgeous man who saw her only as a homely and probably very pathetic old woman.

Her head down, hurrying, she nearly smashed into the young woman coming down the path swinging a shopping bag.

All the things she might never be again. Lovely, radiant, young.

"Cynthia?" She stopped in her tracks and regarded the woman, astounded by what she saw.

Cynthia was dressed in a peek-a-boo sundress of Egyptian cotton dyed a deep rich aqua. The simple lines of the dress showed off the litheness and loveliness of her young body, the length of her slender, flawless legs. Her hair was loose and the sun brought out natural highlights of copper and gold. Her face was sun-kissed, and it showed off the line of her cheekbone and the sweep of her mouth. Her eyes were really quite astonishing, part green and part gold.

Cynthia Forsythe looked gorgeous, not at all like the little bookworm Merry had sat beside at the beach yesterday.

"You look stunning, my dear," Merry said.

"Thank you! I feel wonderful."

"You do?"

"Yes, I do. I've been thinking about your story."

"You have?"

"Yes. You know what bothers me about it?"

"No. What?"

"The daughter! She was so passive. She was hardly even a participant in the story. Everyone else controlled her."

"You don't say," Merry said, but she could feel hope beginning to beat a small tattoo in her chest.

"I've been like her, before, but no more."

"Good for you, my dear," Merry said spiritedly, so much so that she dropped her basket.

"What's that you have there?" Cynthia asked, stooping to pick it up for her. "What a lovely basket. There's champagne in it, but the bottle didn't break."

Lightbulbs were going off like firecrackers in Merry's head. "Isn't that lucky? The basket contains a romantic evening for two, all packaged up."

"Really?" Cynthia breathed.

"Candles, wine, strawberries, chocolates."

"Oh," Cynthia said, her eyes riveted on the contents of the basket.

"Would you like it?" Merry asked softly.

"You'd give it to me?"

"Only if you have someone to share it with."

"I do! I mean, I hope I do. How silly. I mean I do, but I don't even know how to contact him, so…" She tried to hand the basket back, but Merry refused it with a gesture.

"Do you believe in magic?" she asked quietly.

"Well, not really."

"Do you want to?"

"Oh, yes, I do!"

"There's a beach that hardly anyone knows about. Let me tell you where it is. Go there tonight and believe. Wish as hard as you can. You might be amazed by what happens."

"And I might be crushed, too," Cynthia said, but when she left her step was light. She clutched her basket like a girl who wanted desperately to believe in magic.

Merry did something she had not done since she was a little girl. She crossed her fingers as she watched Cynthia go.

She didn't have a cell phone so she had to rush back to her office to call Rick Barnett.

For a long time it seemed as if he wouldn't answer his phone.

But finally he did.

"You should go to that beach again tonight," Merry told him quickly before he had a chance to hang up on her.

"I have other plans," he snarled and hung up on her anyway.

She stared at the phone, and then became aware that the handyman, Alex, was standing in her office door, looking at her, a package of lightbulbs in his hand.

"What?" she snapped. "I don't need any lights fixed."

"Sorry, ma'am. They were just an excuse. I wanted to make sure you were okay," he said. "You seemed distressed earlier."

"Really?" she said, slamming down the phone. He was being nice, but she couldn't even begin to be nice back. "Distressed is correct and that would be because fifty percent of the world's population is male!"

He lifted an eyebrow at her. Oh, he was so good-looking, and so sure of the fact, if she still had a cell phone she'd throw it at him.

"Am I supposed to apologize for that, Ms. Montrose?" he asked. "For the fact that fifty percent of the world's population is male?"

"Oh, get out of my sight you handsome insolent young pup, before I fire you."

He actually had the audacity to wink at her.

And that stupid wink made her feel as if everything in the world might work out after all.

And it made her yearn to be young again. She was willing to bet she'd overlook his low station in life. He still stood in the doorway, regarding her thoughtfully, as if she was a mystery he wanted to solve.

"Go away," she said crabbily. "Please go away. You make my head hurt."

And my heart. And a lot of other places, too.

He left the lightbulbs, backed out the door, and closed it quietly behind him.

It was the first time since he'd arrived in Florida that he'd been cold. But then Rick had been standing in the shrubs outside Cynthia's unit for over two hours. The stupid automatic sprinkler had come on and given him a dousing.

What was he doing here? It was obvious she was out. Probably dancing the night away with the Baron Gruntmunster.

He could go look, hang like a shadow around some of the resort's nightclubs, see where she was. It would not be hard to find someone on an island this size.

He reached into his pocket, before he gave up, and crept onto her balcony to leave another carving there.

It was of a dove. He wasn't even sure what it meant. Hope, he supposed, and soaring joyous flight.

He was stupid to be putting such sentiments into his carvings when real life had already shown him a much harsher reality. Shoving his hands in his pockets, he gave up his vigil and wandered down the walkway.

And then stopped.

What had Merry said to him when she had called him earlier? She'd woken him from a deep and troubled sleep. He'd been annoyed, only half awake.

Go to the beach, she had said.

But he'd had other plans. He'd been planning on waylaying Cynthia at her room, maybe picking up where they had left off last night.

He cursed his own stupidity. Merry knew! She knew who his heart yearned for. It was embarrassing and made him feel vulnerable as hell, but still she knew.

And suddenly he knew why she had told him to go to the beach.

Why that meddlesome old gal!

He moved into a sprint and arrived at the beach just in time to see Cynthia kicking sand over the candles, packing things carefully back in the basket. She was beautiful. The gunnysack beach cover was gone. She was wearing a bikini top and a long tie-on skirt. Both were the color of the sun, brilliant against the inkiness of the night.

"Hello," he said from the shadows.

She started, squinted into the darkness.

"Hello," she said softly.

"Were you expecting someone?"

"No. Yes. You."

"Me?" he breathed.

"Ridiculous, I know. I don't know anything about you, really. Not even your name. Just that you hold people hostage for kisses. And you botch kidnappings."

He moved close to her, thankful the candles were out, thankful for the darkness of the night. The moon was new anyway, and it was overcast.

Darker than pitch out here.

He touched her face, and she closed her eyes. He touched her whole face, slowly, a blind man learning to see. And she never moved beneath the quest of his fingertips, except once to touch his thumb with her lips, to kiss it gently.

"Come swim with me," he said, and his voice was even more hoarse than normal.

"Yes," she said.

And he felt she was saying yes to way more than a swim.

Something in her had opened. As surely as that woman in his carving had been surging out of the sea, as surely as that dove had been soaring up to dance with the sky, Cynthia Forsythe was saying yes to life.

And he was the lucky son of a gun who got to be there as she did it.

She touched the knot that held the skirt at her hip, and it fell away. His mouth went dry. She was feminine perfection, all soft swells and long lines. The wind lifted the honey of her hair.

She was trying to see him, but he knew the moon was still slender enough that he was protected. Or she was. From the worst of it.

His hand found hers, closed around it. There was a feeling of homecoming as they raced hand in hand down to the ocean's edge, out into the waves and plunged into the water.

He heard her laughter and heard his joining it.

He could not remember when he'd last laughed like this. Of course, cloaked in darkness, he could be who he once had been.

He remembered it now—how he had been playful and mischievous. He remembered his energy and his love for life. Rick celebrated who he had once been as he ducked and splashed and swam and hid from her.

And then somehow they were wrapped together, wet skin against wet skin, her hair trailing along his shoulders.

He could feel the luscious curves of her, the sweetness of her breath, the song of her spirit.

And that small flame of hope within his own breast that had been fanned to life since he had first encountered her, flared up. Maybe he was not as destroyed as he had allowed himself to believe.

Not that he could go back and be what he had been before. But perhaps something brand new would emerge. A young man's brashness and confidence would give way to an older man's maturity with a strength that came from having experienced sorrow.

It was as if a spell had been cast on him.

And when she reached up and touched his face, it was broken. Her hands were tender on the scars, but he jerked away from her questing fingertips. He had forgotten, momentarily, that even as a new man he was disfigured, repulsive.

There had been a woman in his life at the time of the accident. Gorgeous, professional, cultured. He had not planned any kind of future with her, but it had still stung unbelievably when he had been able to see he repulsed her. She couldn't look at him after it happened, could barely touch him, had shrunk away from his lips.

Pain burned through him as he remembered.

He put Cynthia aside and swam for the shore.

"Wait," she called. "Don't go, please. I still don't know your name."

But he didn't wait, and he didn't tell her his name.

He was trying to outrun pain, furious, burning, all-consuming.

"I'm going to call you Bear, then."

She was going to call him something, as if she expected she would see him again, as if she was engaged in this relationship whether he wanted to be or not.

He wanted to tell her, no, don't give me a pet name. Don't.

Don't draw me in any deeper, and don't you get in over your head, either. But he could not bring himself to utter those words.

Nor to promise himself he would spare her by never seeing her again.

Cynthia stood in the water and shivered. What had happened? What had she done? One minute their laughter had danced on the night air, the next minute he had gone.

She had touched his face, she realized. She had felt the scarred ridges and known he was wounded.

A few days ago she had known nothing about bears, but now she knew that a wounded bear was the most dangerous animal on the planet.

And the most vulnerable.

She emerged from the water and slowly packed up the wine, the chocolates and the strawberries, still untouched.

A woman with an ounce of good sense would not want to pursue this thing. She was moving into dangerous territory and she knew it.

But all her life she had been afraid. She had chosen, always, the way that was safe, the way that was secure. Isn't that why she had chosen to work for her mother instead of pursuing her own dreams? That way she did not have to fear not making it, did not have to fear failure. She had gained security.

And lost herself.

And somehow that man could lead her back.

She was not taking the safe road this time. She was not selling her soul for the certainty of security. No more.

And when she arrived home and found the carving of the dove on her table outside, it was cemented. She could not stop herself.

She would find out who he was. And for once in her life, Cynthia Forsythe was going after what she wanted.

Danger be damned.

Chapter Six

There, Rick thought, slamming his door behind him and leaning against it with the bone-deep weariness of a man who had run a marathon. He'd fixed it. Even if he couldn't get over his obsession with Cynthia, he was sure he'd fixed it so that she would never want to see him again. He'd left without an excuse and without saying goodbye. She'd always been smart, classy and proud. She wasn't going to put up with that. He hoped.

But before his self-congratulations got too strenuous, he recalled that in their parting moment she had called after him, given him a name—Bear.

That's exactly what he felt like these days. A bear. Holed up in his cave, crabby and reclusive. Bears didn't see that well, either.

Restless, he picked up a piece of carving wood. He could see the shape of the bear in it, could almost feel it emerging from under his knife. But it would be a bigger piece than he normally did, and his mood wasn't right for it.

Instead, he turned to his sketchbook, opened it up and stared at the rough drawing of the stairs and floor for the chapel that he had drawn.

Despite how little was there, it was good. Real. Capturing exactly that mystical "something" that he was trying to capture.

And then he thought of swimming with Cynthia, of her laughter filling the air, and of how that carefree time together had made him feel. Young again.

As if her laughter—her laughter, not to mention the taste of her lips, the press of her sweet, wet curves into him—could heal something in him. Lift him above the pain.

That's what being with her did. It made him feel hope.

And wasn't that what love did? Made people feel hope beyond what they probably had any right to feel?

Still, if you were going to draw it, if you were going to put that feeling into a building, how would you do it?

His pencil seemed to work on its own. Before he knew it, his exhaustion was gone and walls were sitting on those granite floors, but walls like nothing he had ever built or even seen before. They were walls made of glass.

He looked at the drawing and felt his breath stop. The concept was beautiful. Probably impossible to execute, but beautiful.

He snorted. "It's Florida. The average temperature here is eighty-five degrees, day in and day out. People would cook in a chapel made of glass."

Well, not necessarily. The huge tree that sheltered the clearing would help reduce the heat if he could manage to save it. And there was amazing technology. There were argon-gas-filled windows that let in light but filtered out heat.

And wasn't that what hope did? Let in the light and filtered out all else?

Was it possible to build something like this? Of course it was. Greenhouses were built on this concept. He fiddled, did some math, figured out some bearings, figured some more. The glass would not stand on its own. It would have to fit into a framework. How could he make the framework seem nearly invisible?

The challenge engrossed him completely. When he finished, hours had slipped away from him and he was aware of feeling a way he had not felt for a long time. Passionate. Fully engaged in life.

Excited. And he knew he had one person to thank for that, and he had treated her badly.

He looked again at the piece of wood that spoke of a bear and rejected it for a smaller lighter piece.

The dolphin took shape of its own volition, joyous, leaping from the water, playing with the elements.

That was what Cynthia had given him tonight, a spirit of play. He peeked out of his eternally closed drapes and realized morning had come. He looked at his watch. He had been so engrossed, first in the walls of the chapel and then in the carving of the dolphin that he had lost track of time. More important, he had lost track of himself. He had been free, for a while, from the pain of loss. It had not even crossed his mind that he was scarred or blinded in one eye or that his larynx had been crushed or that he was haunted by dreams of being trapped and crushed under a pressing weight.

It was too late to go there now, to Cynthia, with dawn already strong, but tonight, he would leave her the gift of the dolphin. He didn't have to see her. He didn't have to engage her anymore in his life.

It was a thank-you and a farewell.

"Of course," he told himself gruffly, "I think you've said that before."

And he actually laughed at himself.

Cynthia awoke feeling as if she had a hangover. When she remembered some of the details of the night before it occurred to her a hangover was a distinct possibility. She had come home and put her vow to live dangerously into practice by drinking that whole bottle of champagne by herself.

"What a pathetic thing to do," she scolded herself. She had left the beach feeling so brave, so determined.

But with each sip of that wine, instead of becoming braver, her determination had faltered. You couldn't *chase* a man. You couldn't throw yourself at him if he wasn't interested. Where was her pride? Plus, you especially couldn't pursue him if you didn't even know who he was, or exactly how to find him.

Something rustled near her fingertips, and she sat up and groaned. Chocolate wrappers. She had polished those off, too. The wrappers littered her bed.

Memories of the rest of the evening, after her disastrous departure from Bear, crowded into a mind that had not invited them. Oh, yes, after half the bottle of champagne she had hunted for *Hot Desert Kisses,* finally finding the book under the sofa cushion where she had tucked it, in a sober moment, to keep her mind off kisses of any sort at all.

So, barreling toward full-blown inebriation, she had finished off the book, not to mention every single one of those chocolates.

Had the book been trashy? No! It had been glorious. She had been weeping volumes and stuffing back chocolates at an alarming rate for the last three pages.

Now someone knocked on her door, and she pulled her pillow over her head. She was tired of being woken up by mysterious knocks. She was tired of hoping it was him. She was tired of her excruciatingly boring life. She was tired of the fact that it kept promising to be something else and instead left her feeling more deflated and pathetic than before.

Her determination to live with more verve faltered in light of the fact that her first spontaneous decision—to polish off the champagne on her own—had left her nursing the most horrible headache of her entire life.

Reasonable people knew that's what living dangerously did!

The knock came again. Her mother coming over to call a truce? Jerome again?

What if it was the mystery man?

"I don't care if it is him," she told herself, but of course she did.

What would it hurt to get up and just take a tiny peek out of her security peephole? She tiptoed to the door and pressed her eye to it. Merry Montrose stood there. Cynthia held her breath and hoped the woman would go away. But she didn't. She knocked and then she knocked again.

Muttering under her breath, Cynthia finally opened the door. "What?" she asked, and could hear the surliness in her own voice.

"It must be contagious," Merry said cheerfully.

"What?"

"A certain crabbiness in the air. Especially in the mornings."

Cynthia was aware of Merry's sharp eyes taking in her appearance. She could guess exactly how she looked. She probably still had a ring of chocolate around her mouth. She tried to look dignified and not at all haggard and hung-over. She suspected she failed from the look of concern on Merry's face.

"Are you feeling all right, my dear?"

"Not particularly," Cynthia said.

"Your romantic evening?" Merry ventured, her eyes searching for and finding the basket, which was lying topsy-turvy beside the couch.

And then she saw the champagne bottle lying on its side, empty, on the coffee table.

"There was no romantic evening," Cynthia said. "I mean there was the start of one but I finished it by myself. I hate that man. Whoever he is." What she really hated was all the things he made her feel—self-doubt, then soaring confidence, then more self-doubt. Hope and then the letdown of things hoped for not happening. She hated how she was evaluating a perfectly respectable life—her life—as if her choices had all been rotten and wrong for her.

"Hate him?" Merry said, uneasily. "I would hope that's a little, er, strong."

"Ha. Not nearly strong enough."

"But the wine—" she ventured.

"I drank it by myself. And ate all the chocolates. And the strawberries. Don't tell my mother." She could have kicked herself for saying that, as if she needed her mother's approval, but she simply wasn't in her best form. "Never mind. I don't want to discuss last evening. Or my romantic endeavors or lack thereof. Or my mother."

"Oh," Merry said. "Are those things linked in some way?"

"I hope not," Cynthia said dejectedly. "Is there something I can help you with?" *Quickly, so that I can go back to bed, pull my pillow over my head and suffocate myself.*

Merry looked momentarily confused, as if she had totally forgotten what brought her knocking on the door at the ungodly hour of—Cynthia slid her eyes to the clock—ten-thirty. And then she smiled. "Oh, yes, I've come to deliver an invitation."

It was him, Cynthia thought, and felt her traitorous heart pick up tempo. This was his style exactly. Use a middleman, build the intrigue and excitement! She could feel the excitement building even as she ordered herself, that no matter what the invitation was, she must say no. All that excitement kept building only to end in a big fat zero. Much more of that kind of stress and she would end up addicted to romance novels. She could probably live without the chocolate and champagne, but without hot, hungry kisses?

"Do you remember meeting Parris at the dress shop the other day?" Merry asked her. "She told me you shopped together and had so much fun."

Oh, yes, Parris, who encouraged red and sexy things.

But what did Parris have to do with her mystery man?

"She told you she was getting married, didn't she?"

"Of course," Cynthia said, and tried not to feel envious of the other woman's obvious love. Parris shone—her skin glowed with it, her eyes danced, she walked with the unconscious sensuous sway of a woman who was adored. Parris was way beyond all the confusing fun-and-games part of a courtship.

Though so far, Cynthia thought cynically, she had not had a courtship, plenty of games but no fun.

Except for last night, when they had played like dolphins in the black silk of a calm sea. And he had wrapped himself around her and kissed her...

"Er, Cynthia, did you hear me?"

"Sorry. No." She was blushing. "What did you say?"

"Parris and Brad are getting married here at the resort

in a very private ceremony. It's too bad the new chapel won't be done."

"The new chapel?" Cynthia asked.

"You haven't even got that far yet?"

"How far?" she asked, confused.

"Oh, never mind," Merry said obviously flustered. "I just thought by now, if things were progressing—"

"I'm not following you. What things? What progression?"

"Forgive me," Merry said, rattled. "I'm just an old woman. I get dotty sometimes, mumble away to myself, stomp on cell phones that I need desperately."

"Oh," Cynthia said with real sympathy. The woman did seem very flustered. "Well, thank you for telling me about Brad and Parris. Now, if you'll excuse me."

"Oh, my apologies. I'm not done delivering the invitation! The ceremony is small and private, as I said, but they are planning quite the gala afterward. It will be outdoors and spectacular, naturally, since I'm helping with the arrangements. Parris asked me if I could track you down. She so wanted you to be there."

"Me?" Cynthia asked, surprised and flattered. "Parris hardly knows me."

"I don't think a person would have to know you very well to like you, Cynthia. You sparkle."

"Me?"

"Yes. Didn't you know? And I think you and Parris have quite a bit in common."

Ha. Parris is madly in love, and I'm madly in limbo.

"You're both young women on the brink of discovering the full joys of life."

"I wish," Cynthia muttered, but still she took the details for Parris and Brad's reception, time and place. Oh, how she would love to bring her mystery man there. As far as she knew, her mother didn't know Parris, so she wouldn't be there, looking on, making judgments.

She could almost hear her. "Darling, his manners." And "What's wrong with his face?"

No, they could be normal. Have a few drinks, dance, laugh, talk.

They could get to know each other as if it were a real date.

But would he come into the light? Would he have to? At an outdoor gathering at night, surely there would be plenty of places where the lighting would be more subtle.

Of course, there was still the challenge of finding him. How simple that had seemed, last night, emerging from the water, full of the energy and sizzle of his kisses. But now her energy had fizzled. Besides, her head hurt.

No wonder her mother enjoyed a good migraine so much! It was a great excuse to completely abscond on life!

In the harsh glare of early morning, with her head pounding unreasonably, Cynthia was not nearly so certain of what was possible, what was plausible, what was reality and what was just hopeful fantasy.

"So, may I tell her you'll come?" Merry said.

"I don't know. I don't want to go by myself."

"Ask someone."

"It's more complicated than that."

"That's what I was afraid of," Merry said. "Hardly any progress at all." Her attention wandered and then stopped on the carvings that Cynthia had displayed on her table.

"My gosh," she said, and pushed right past Cynthia. "These are beautiful. I have always wanted to start an art gallery here that would showcase exactly this kind of work. I'm afraid I have neither the expertise nor, at the moment, the enthusiasm."

Merry wanted to start an art gallery? Here? Wouldn't that

be Cynthia's dream job? To find wonderful one-of-a-kind pieces of art to fill a gallery in a beautiful place like this?

Last night, emerging from the water, anything had seemed possible. She probably would have said to Merry, look no further, I'm the one for the job. But today…well, today, everything seemed different. Her old world seemed like a much safer place than this one. It might not have been exciting, but it had not had all these painful ups and downs, either.

"Exquisite," Merry said, touching the carvings again.

"They are beautiful, aren't they?" Cynthia said, and tried to quell the dreamy note in her voice.

She could tell she failed because Merry slid her a look of sly interest.

"Where did you get them?"

Cynthia hesitated. "Someone leaves them for me. In the night."

"Really?" Merry breathed. "Like the legend?"

"Well, of course not like that," Cynthia said, blushing. "Not exactly like that. I mean he hasn't crept into my room and, you know."

Merry looked askance.

"I mean I haven't given him the gift of myself or anything."

"Oh, I see! Still," Merry said, and her vague expression was gone. She was smiling like a Cheshire cat.

"I don't even know if it's a man leaving those things," Cynthia sputtered defensively.

"Of course it's a man," Merry said.

"Well, if it is, I would like to know who."

"Would you?"

"Yes!"

"Well, then wait for him. Do you think these little items are appearing by magic? Poof, a carving appears?"

"You're the one who encouraged me to believe in magic!"

"I know, but with some limits. It's not *Bewitched,* you know. People can't just move items with a twitch of their nose. At least not usually."

"What are you saying?"

"You college-educated girls can be so dim, really."

It was said with such kindly exasperation that somehow Cynthia could not be offended.

"If you want to see who is delivering these wonderful treasures, lie in wait. Set a trap."

"Of course," Cynthia breathed. There was that hope again, fluttering in her breast like a bird that wanted out. She tried to quell it. "But that would assume he's coming back, that there are more gifts for me."

Merry picked up the carving of the woman and then the one of the dove. She held it for a long time.

Cynthia felt as if the elderly woman could feel the artist's spirit rising up through the wood as surely as Cynthia herself had been able to.

"Of course he's coming back," Merry said with soft certainty. "Of course there will be more gifts."

"So, what do I do if I catch him?"

"Child, are you completely hopeless in the romance department?"

Cynthia nodded solemnly.

"You've never wooed a man before?"

Cynthia shook her head.

"Invite him to attend Parris's celebration with you. It would be perfect."

Cynthia took a deep breath. She caught a glimpse of the woman she had been last night, coming out of the water. "All right, if I catch him, I will."

"Not if," Merry corrected her, "when." She waltzed out the door, whistling.

Whistling!

It wasn't until the door was closed that Cynthia realized whatever remnants of a hangover she'd had were completely gone.

Hours later, dressed in black and crouched in the bushes beside her terrace, Cynthia found that her confidence that her mystery man would appear had dissolved as completely as her hangover. This was not nearly as fun or as exciting as they made it look in the movies. She was cramped, she was cold and she was tired. She had to go to the bathroom. She had neglected to put on a watch, but she was sure it was well past midnight.

He had come at dawn the time he had left the figurine of the woman, and she was almost positive she could not wait that long.

Not even for love.

She was ready to abandon her post when she heard a sound. Was she making it up? No, there was definitely someone else in the shrubs, moving stealthily toward her terrace.

She had an awful thought. What if it wasn't him? A cat burglar! What good pickings there would be at a resort like this, where people of great wealth let their guards down so completely. She shrank back.

And then she saw a dark form so close to her she could nearly touch him. Relief filled her.

She knew it was him. She was not sure how, but she knew. Perhaps it was his scent, playing on the breeze, warm and masculine. Or the power in his stance, or his ease with the darkness.

Amused now, she watched as he made his way out of

the shrubs, hesitated on her terrace, then reached into his pocket and pulled out the gift. She waited until he had placed it, watching as he stood there.

She could not see his face. She could only vaguely see his body, the silhouette of it dark and powerful. But she saw his hesitation and wanting. Wanting that matched her own.

She waited until he had come off the patio and was moving stealthily away. She crept up behind him, and he froze, sensing her seconds before she spoke.

"Don't turn around," she ordered him. The tension eased from the set of his shoulders.

"All right. Can you tell me why?"

"Certainly," she said. "This is a kidnapping." And she reached into the back pocket of her brand-new hip-hugging black jeans and removed the silk scrap from it.

She reached up, and she had to stand on tiptoe to fasten it around his head and cover his eyes. As she placed it her fingers skimmed the patch that covered his left eye.

As well as being scarred, he was partially blind, then. Was that why he didn't want her to see him? But it was romantic! Didn't he know that? That eye patch made him like a swashbuckler of old.

Still, some sixth sense told her to honor his sensitivity to his handicap. Staying behind him, she whispered instructions to him, how to move, what small hazards to avoid.

She loved being behind him, allowed to study the sweep of his shoulders, the pantherlike grace of his walk, allowed to touch his elbow and be so close to him she could feel the warmth radiating off his body.

Finally, they arrived at the beach where he had abandoned her the night before. She pressed her hands on his shoulders until he sat in the sand. She stayed behind, removed the silk cloth, then settled beside him. She tried to read his profile but the night seemed darker than ever. She could not tell if he was young or old, handsome or homely.

And oddly, she didn't care about any of those things. "So," she said, "tell me about you."

"Aren't you going to lecture me about leaving you last night? It was dastardly."

She laughed. "How can you lecture a man who uses a word like *dastardly?*" She took a chance. "And wears an eye patch. Are you a pirate?"

"No."

"Convince me. You have stolen kisses. Tell me who you are."

"What do you want to know first?"

Everything seemed too small. Besides, she didn't want to know what he did for a living and she didn't want to know if he was a college graduate. She didn't want to know if he owned a house, or had a membership at a privileged golf club.

Those were the things her mother would want to know.

She wanted to know his heart.

How did you know a man's heart?

"What's your favorite constellation?" she asked on an impulse.

He laughed, startled. "You can't even see the stars tonight. It's too overcast. But if you could, I would look for Orion, the hunter. When I look at the sky and see him, I feel the antiquity of the universe and the timelessness of beauty. I feel humbled by how all the best things are unchanging. The stars, the mountains, the sea. And you? Your favorite constellation?"

"Orion, too," she said, feeling the thrill of his answer. It was as if she knew him, knew his soul and his heart, and his words had just confirmed her knowing. "Orion is the only one I know, really. I mean the Milky Way and the Big and Little Dipper, but Orion—when I was a little girl, my father would spin wonderful tales around him, tell me what he was hunting and why. He made up whole exciting lives for Orion."

"And what is your favorite flower?" he asked her.

She heard the hunger in his voice to know her in the very same way she wanted to know him.

Not in the what-do-you-do-for-a-living way. Not in the small-talk-in-the-bar way.

He wanted to know her heart and she thrilled to the realization.

"Tulips," she said without hesitation.

He laughed.

"What's funny?" she demanded.

"I don't know. I expected you to say orchids. I kind of picture you as a white rose—beauty and innocence combined."

"What makes you say innocent?" she demanded, faintly peeved. Their kisses had been scorching in her mind.

"I don't know. Do I sense a certain lack of, um, experience?"

"No," she lied, and his easy laughter let her know she had not pulled it off.

"So, why tulips?" he asked.

"Because of how early they grow, practically popping up through the snow, so hardy and so resilient. I feel like they bring hope."

"Funny you should mention that word," he said, almost to himself, but then retreated quickly from that place. His tone became light again. "Do you want to know my favorite flower? You can't laugh."

"I won't."

"I love dandelions."

"No!" She did laugh.

"Yeah. I haven't always. But I do now, because of a

story I heard. You know those ones people send you on the Internet?"

"Tell me." She loved the soft rasp of his voice. She felt as if she could listen to it forever.

"A man from Barbados was visiting his son-in-law and daughter in the U.S. for the first time. He had arrived in the darkness, and in the morning the son-in-law was dismayed to see his new father-in-law at the window staring at his lawn. He was so embarrassed. He hadn't had time to mow. The dandelions had taken over. And then before he could apologize for the mess, his father-in-law turned to him and said, "So beautiful, a lawn of pure sunshine. It must take you forever to plant all those flowers.""

She laughed with delight.

"So, I've decided I like them, too. They remind me that everything is perspective. Everything. So little is really true, it's only as we think it."

And so the night went. They talked about flowers and philosophy and art and books. She told him once she had dreamed of being an artist, and even now she sometimes thought heaven would be running a small gallery. She told him about her work for her mother, and her creeping dissatisfaction, sentiments she had never expressed to anyone. They talked until she felt her voice was growing hoarse from it.

Then, the night sky lightened, barely discernable, but she felt him stiffen beside her. She realized her voice was hoarse because she had done most of the talking. He had revealed little of himself.

She could see the patch over his eye, and she could see the scars, though barely, because the night was still so thick around them. But while her eyes saw, her heart felt—felt his great aloneness, his enormous strength, his vulnerability.

"Stay and watch the sun come up with me." She wanted to see all of him, in the full light. She wanted her acceptance to wash over him like a balm.

"I can't."

"Why?"

"I fear I am like those dandelions, sweet lady. Most people would find me ugly."

"Perhaps their perceptions are wrong," she said.

"Perhaps," he agreed, but she heard the sadness in his voice.

"Trust me?" she asked, pleading.

"Not just yet, sweet lady," he said. "Close your eyes."

She did, and he kissed her with such tenderness it could break her heart.

"Tell me your name," she said.

"Bear will do. And yours?"

"Cynthia." But she felt disappointed he was trusting her with nothing, not even his name.

"Are you married?" she asked suddenly.

"No," he said, the insult of the question ringing in his voice.

"Then why all the secretiveness?"

He was silent for a long time. "Do you know what the hardest thing is for a man?" he asked, finally.

"No."

"Admitting fear."

Fear she could understand. Had she not spent most of her life afraid? Afraid of the unknown? Afraid of disappointing those she loved? Afraid of striking out on her own instead of staying with her mother where everything was safe and predictable?

"Good night, sweet lady." His lips touched hers again, and then he was gone.

"Bear! Wait!"

For a moment she thought he would not answer. But he did.

"Cynthia?"

"There's a wedding celebration. Two nights from now. Will you come with me?"

"I can't."

"It's outdoors. I'm sure we could find a place where the light was low. Please?"

"How can I refuse you?" he asked, tormented. "How?"

"Then don't."

"I have to think about it. Two nights from now?"

"Yes."

"Will you meet me right here tomorrow, at this same time and I will give you my answer?"

Her heart leapt, for she might not have a future, or a date for Parris and Brad's reception, but at least she had tomorrow.

She walked home alone, but when she got there, she found the carving of the dolphin waiting for her on her outdoor table. As she traced its dancing joyous lines with her fingertips, it felt as if she wasn't alone at all.

She looked at it and knew exactly what it represented. That night they had swum together, the freedom and joy the water and the night had given them. She clutched it to her breast and fiddled with the lock on her door.

She came into her suite to find her mother just opening the adjoining door.

"Oh, sorry, Cynthia. I was worried about you. Where have you been?"

Falling in love. "Here and there," she told her mother vaguely.

"My God, look at the time. It's nearly three in the

morning. And you look like a cat burglar, all dressed in black like that. Have I seen those slacks before? Jeans, aren't they?"

Jeans was said in a tone she usually reserved for *cockroaches*.

"Mother, I'm exhausted. Could we talk later?"

"Jerome told me I must stop prying into your life. Cynthia, he said I was the mother from hell! That isn't true, is it?"

"Of course not."

"Then can I pry?"

"No."

Her mother sighed. "Cynthia, it's very hard for me to mind my own business!"

"Why don't you tell me what you've been doing these last few days," Cynthia said to distract her, sinking onto the sofa and patting the spot beside her.

Her mother told her eagerly. Cynthia was not even sure if Emma was aware that every sentence contained the word *Jerome* at least once.

"Tonight we met the loveliest young couple. They're getting married on Thursday, and they were gracious enough to invite us to the reception."

"Really?" Cynthia said, hoping the lateness of the hour would help her mother overlook the woodenness of her tone.

"Why, Parris said she knew you! And that you were going, too."

"Maybe."

"I hope this means I finally get to meet this mystery man of yours. There is a man, isn't there? I mean I'm not prying! Just reading all the signs."

But Cynthia's spirit felt as though it was sinking like a stone.

She had told Bear he could trust her.

But now she wondered how true that was. Because she did not want him to be subjected to her mother's judgments.

And why was that?

Because her mother would never in a million years tell her to choose a man with palms that were rough. Oh, no. The exact opposite might be true. She would look down on a man with rough working hands. And a patch over his eye. And a voice as rough as ridged concrete.

Everything was so new. Was it strong enough to withstand the winds of disapproval? Was she?

Chapter Seven

The transition from the otherworldly peace and tranquility of La Torchere to the harsh lights and relentless activity of the emergency ward made Cynthia's head throb.

Though given the size of the lump on her head, it would very likely have been throbbing, anyway.

"Just a little while longer," the white-clad nurse told Cynthia with a cheery smile. "Sorry for the wait, but we've just had a car accident. The whole family is in, poor things."

It wasn't that Cynthia didn't have sympathy for the family who had been in the car accident. It was just that she had some place to be.

She pressed the cloth to her aching forehead, snuck another look at the clock, and moaned. She cursed her stupidity and bad luck. She had stumbled over a table in her room and cracked her head open.

"Are you all right?" her mother asked solicitously, then glared at the busy nurse.

"Oh, never better," Cynthia said, heard the snap and sarcasm in her own voice and felt too trapped and out of sorts to be ashamed of it.

At this very moment, she was supposed to be with her Bear. He was going to give her his answer tonight about the wedding, though she knew his answer would reflect more than whether or not they were going to a wedding celebration together.

It would reflect whether they were moving forward, as a couple, chancing commitment in small ways. It would reflect whether or not the little thrill of possessiveness she felt when using the phrase *her* Bear, had any basis at all in reality.

No, the event itself—Parris and Brad's wedding—really wasn't the important part. Though the thought of attending an event that affirmed the power of love and the existence of romance would be wonderful, it was Bear's answer that was important.

Which was why Cynthia had been thinking about changing plans. Once he said yes to the wedding, she'd tell him it wasn't that important. Men hated weddings, anyway, didn't they? Cynthia didn't want to be any place with Bear if her mother was going to be there. How fun would that be, trying to duck her mother all night? She didn't have to dread the mommy test if there wasn't going to be one.

Still, regardless of his answer about the wedding, they could have had tonight. They should have had tonight. Her heart warmed at the thought of one more night with him— talking, swimming, laughing. Kissing.

The remembrance of his kisses made her shiver.

"Are you going to faint?" her mother asked. "Jerome, do you think Cynthia is going to faint?"

"I don't think so," he said calmly.

"I'm not going to faint, Mother, honestly. I have a scratch on my head. We shouldn't wait here a moment longer. These people are busy with real emergencies."

They shouldn't wait because at this very moment Bear would be sliding from the treeline onto the beach, all dark grace and powerful masculine mystique.

Cynthia was so drawn by the picture, by her need to be with him, that she rose to her feet.

It was Jerome, not her mother, who put a hand on her forearm, and pushed her gently back down.

"You really need to have a doctor look at that," he said firmly.

She glanced again at the clock, feeling almost frantic. He would be looking around now, wondering where she was, scanning the walkways for her. Maybe he would be settling in the sand, looking out over the water.

And Cynthia was on the mainland! In the emergency room of a Fort Myers hospital, her forehead laid open wide, with not one single way of getting word to the man who waited for her.

"A few stitches and you'll be just fine," that cheery nurse had told her an hour ago, showing her how to hold the compress until they got to her.

"That is a truly nasty wound," she had noted, in the same cheery voice. "How did you do that?"

It was the question Cynthia least wanted to be asked. She had decided she wasn't telling anyone the truth. Because one truth could not be told without the other…

This afternoon, she had decided to see just what kind of handicap it was to have sight in only one eye. How debilitating could that be? Perhaps knowing that could help her unlock some of Bear's mystery, his reticence about being seen.

So, out of cotton batting and medical tape, Cynthia had made herself a makeshift patch and secured it over her left eye.

Actually, for the first half hour or so, it hadn't seemed that bad. She was rereading a few of her favorite parts of *Hot Desert Kisses*. She felt faintly disoriented, not tragically handicapped. But after the first half hour she had noticed she felt dizzy, as if the words were running together on the page and she was straining to make sense of them. She had put the book down and gone to plug in the kettle for tea. She noticed she was not nearly as confident as she would normally be. There was a slightly off-kilter feeling and it took her two stabs to actually insert the kettle plug in the wall.

And then the phone had rung, and she had gone to get it from where she had left it beside her on the sofa in the living room.

That simple.

She had totally missed the coffee table on her left-hand side. It had been completely in her blind spot. She had tripped hard and fallen on the corner of it. For a moment, she had just lain there, stunned. And then she had touched her forehead. The skin was peeled back like a banana and her hand came away red with her own blood.

Her mother did not handle crisis well, and Cynthia had been lying on the floor feeling intensely foolish and debating what to do when her mother had the awful timing to come through the adjoining door.

The blood might have indicated quite a bit more severe an injury than it really was, because the resulting hysterics had brought the island equivalent of 9-1-1.

And a quick trip on La Torchere's private plane into the medical facilities at Fort Myers.

"Why were you wearing that patch over your eye?" her mother said again, sitting beside her in the emergency room, taking her hand and squeezing it.

"I told you. I got something in my eye. It was watering like crazy, so I covered it up."

When had she become such an accomplished liar? Well, maybe not that accomplished, because her mother kept asking the same question over and over again, her tone edged with disbelief.

"But why didn't you just pop over to my place if you had a lash, or something, in your eye? I could have fixed it in just a jiffy. Even if I am the mother from hell, I can still be counted on to—"

"Bluebird, dear, leave the girl alone. She isn't six."

"She may not be six, but she's is acting very strangely these days," her mother said, a trifle defensively. "Being a concerned parent does not make me the mother from hell."

Her mother had latched on to the mother-from-hell title with a kind of fierce fascination. She seemed bent on convincing the world—Cynthia and Jerome—she was completely undeserving of such a name.

"Didn't you say you were thinking of doing a book on the Underground Railroad?" Jerome asked, artfully changing the subject and giving Cynthia a reassuring wink. "Look, here's an article about that very thing."

Thank God for Jerome's steadying presence, and the effortless way he diverted her mother.

But not even he could do anything about the line-up and emergencies far more urgent than hers. Having occupied her mother, Jerome went to find a coffee machine while Cynthia counted the ticking of seconds on the clock.

"We're at the last layer on a cast, and then you're next,"

the nurse told her, bustling by. Then she stopped and shook her head. Far away Cynthia could hear what she heard.

Sirens.

"You *were* next," the nurse said with an apologetic smile.

Again, Cynthia had to fight back the wild desire to leap to her feet, throw away the compress they had given her with strict instructions to keep the pressure on, and head out that door. She had an appointment! If she didn't show what would he do? What would he think?

The emergency-room doors flew open and a stretcher went by.

"Gunshot wound," one of the attendants bellowed.

Cynthia groaned to keep from crying.

Rick sat on the deserted beach. He had a white rose beside him, which was looking more wilted by the second. The moments had ticked away, and with them had gone that exquisite tickle of anticipation he had been feeling about seeing her again.

So, she had come to her senses. Cynthia wasn't coming. It was a good thing, really, if he thought about it rationally, not that he'd had a thought that would qualify as rational for some time now.

They were supposed to have met two hours ago. The rational thing would have been to go home.

But no, he sat here in the darkness, feeling an aching hopefulness that kept him glued to his spot in the sand as if it had turned to cement around him. In the city he might have allowed himself to indulge in any number of excuses for her: traffic, an accident, a family emergency.

But all those things seemed as if they could not happen here in this magical place that seemed to be returning him to himself.

Would he wait until dawn? Did he have anything better to do?

He heard the sound behind him and leapt to his feet, startled, and a thorn from the rose bit into one hand. He sucked the drop of blood and watched. She was coming across the sand toward him, emerging from the darkness like a vision. But all did not seem well. Was she staggering?

Was she drunk? Cynthia drunk? No, impossible. She was always composed, in control. Still, he did not move toward her, trying to figure out what was wrong.

"You're still here," she said, and he could hear the tears in her voice and the slur.

"What is it?" he asked.

"Is that rose for me?"

Her speech was off. What on earth was wrong with her?

"Yes, for you."

She took it and regarded it solemnly. "Innocence and beauty." She remembered, but there was a hazy edge to her voice.

Then she dropped the rose, flung herself against him and wept.

He held her for a long time, allowing himself to feel simple gratitude because she had come. He let her warmth seep into him, making him aware of how cold he had become. Not just tonight. His life had become cold, and Cynthia promised warmth, drawing him like a moth to a flame. But would the end result be just as disastrous?

He took her shoulders, tipped her away and looked into her face, knowing he would see her better than she could see him. Her eyes had a glazed look. And then he saw the white bandage, underneath the fringe of her hair.

"What on earth is going on, Cynthia?"

When she didn't answer, he gently pried up the edge of

the bandage. There was a huge lump on her head, and it was crisscrossed with stitches.

She swayed against him.

"They wanted to keep me in the hospital," she wailed. "They thought they should watch for a concussion."

"You've had an accident?" So much for La Torchere being out of the reach of the real world, a valuable lesson for him. Bad things happened here, too.

"A small mishap," she agreed sadly.

"You should be in the hospital, and you're here?"

"Nothing could have kept me from being here."

Flattering as that was, he was furious with her. She had jeopardized her personal safety for a clandestine meeting on the beach with a man who was so unworthy?

"What happened?" he asked her sternly.

"I fell. Bumped my head."

The girl was swaying on her feet! He dealt with the anger he felt at her putting herself at risk like this by scooping her up in his arms.

"You are going straight to bed," he snapped.

She missed the impatience entirely! "You're so masterful," she said groggily.

"Have you been reading romance novels?" he asked sternly.

She giggled helplessly.

"Are you on something?"

"No, no. Just a little morphine."

"Just a little morphine," he muttered. "And a little head injury. You can barely walk and barely talk and you're out traipsing around in the dark? Are you insane?"

"I think I might be," she admitted. "Feels so good."

She rubbed her cheek sleepily on his shirt. That felt pretty good, too.

He sighed. "Cynthia, you should have stayed at the hospital if that's what the doctor wanted."

"I didn't want you to think I wouldn't come. I couldn't let you think that!"

"Ah, Cynthia." He could feel the fury melting out of him as she cuddled in closer. Her body was limp and relaxed, and the delicious warmth of her was like a drug.

"What did you do to yourself, sweet lady?" *And what are you doing to me?*

"Dumb," she mumbled. "I stumbled, hit my head on the coffee table. Split my forehead wide open. Look like Frankenstein's monster, now."

"You couldn't look like Frankenstein's monster if you dyed yourself green and your head was held on with screws."

"Frankenstein's bride, then," she said stubbornly. "You won't want to go to the wedding with me."

Now didn't seem like a particularly good time to tell her he had decided not to go, anyway. And it wasn't that he didn't want to go. It's that he wanted it too much. He wanted every thing and every moment she was prepared to give him.

And that in itself was a good enough reason to say, no, let's back off a bit, let's give it a rest.

But did she really think he was that shallow? That he would refuse to be seen with her because of the way she looked?

He, of all people, knew how that felt. To be rejected, thrown back, because of scars or imperfections.

"Did you forget my rose?" she asked as he strode toward her apartment.

"Yes. Never mind. I'll get you another one."

"I want that one," she said in a small voice. "Please?"

He swore under his breath, which she thought was masterful, again. She kissed his chest. He went back for the rose, nearly broke his back hanging on to her and bending over in the sand to retrieve it, then stuffed it unceremoniously in his pocket.

"Doesn't that hurt?" she asked.

"Yes," he said as the thorns stabbed him.

Cradling her weight carefully, and trying to ignore the rose jabbing him, he made his way to her door, looked around carefully and opened the handle. It was unlocked, more uncharacteristically reckless behavior on her part.

He set her down carefully, not wanting to trip over the coffee table. It was even darker in here than outside, which was plenty dark. Even so he noticed an adjoining door, sensed the threat of interruption.

"Where does that go?"

"Mommy dearest," she said with a cackle.

"That's what I was afraid of." He went through the blackness and locked the door.

She mewed approvingly. He hoped she wasn't getting any ideas about what it meant, because he was not so callous that he would seduce a woman under the influence of morphine.

Surely they didn't use morphine for a few stitches? But there was no sense pursuing it. It was obvious she didn't have a clue what they had used or why.

He took her hand and then her shoulders and guided her through the darkness to her bedroom. The bedroom was a mirror image of his. So why did hers seem so different? Feminine and sensual and like a siren calling a sailor to the rocks?

He set her on the edge of the bed. In his imagination, in weak moments, it was true, he had thought of this moment. Only it hadn't been anything like this! He had been taking her lips in his, thrusting her back on the quilt...

Don't go there, he ordered himself firmly and pulled back the bedclothes like a nanny getting a child ready for bed. "Come on, in you go."

He turned back to her. She was still on the edge of the bed, but she had her shirt half on and half over her head. She looked as if she was hopelessly stuck.

"Ouch, that hurts. Forget my head," she said, from somewhere inside the tangle of that shirt.

"Yeah, well, I seem to be losing mine, too."

She had fully exposed the lace of her bra, the gentle swell of her breasts mounding over those exquisite lace cups. Her skin looked like silk, and he could smell the delightful feminine fragrance of her.

He gently pulled the shirt back down. Trying not to touch, yearning to touch, he finally got the shirt back where it belonged.

"I need my pajamas," she told him mutinously.

"I'll pull off your shoes. No pajamas."

"No pajamas?" she said with slurred wickedness.

"Lord, have mercy," he said with feeling. "I didn't mean it like that. You can sleep in your clothes tonight."

"Want you to see them."

"What?" he asked, the panic evident in his voice. "You want me to see what?"

"Pajamas."

"Not a good idea." He watched her mouth form the most adorable little pout and tried to placate her. "Maybe I did see them once. Bunnies?"

"Not those ones."

"That's what I was afraid of. Cynthia, be a good girl, and get under the covers."

"Tired of being a good girl."

"Well, your timing couldn't be worse." He was trying

so darned hard to be a good guy, to be worthy of her, to act like a gentleman and not the kid from the wrong side of the tracks.

She really didn't have much fight in her. She was further gone than she wanted to admit. It took only the slightest shove to lie her down. He pulled the blankets over her and tucked them under her chin. It was way too warm in here for that kind of covering, but either she was going to be too warm or he was.

And she didn't even know what universe she was in at the moment.

"Okay. You're all settled. Need anything else? A glass of water? An aspirin?"

"Don't go," she said, her eyes huge on his face. For a minute he wondered how well she could see him, but decided if it was that well she certainly wouldn't be asking him to stay.

"Uh, I can't stay." She was really asking a little much of him. But he made no move to leave. Instead, he leaned closer and looked at her wound. Her eyes were shut and gentle little sputters were starting to emerge from her lips.

He was amazed she had made it to the beach in this state, even more amazed it had mattered enough to her.

Which is why he could not go to that wedding. She would be disappointed. He did not want to hurt her. She already appeared to care way, way too much.

She drifted, and then her eyes fluttered open. She started awake and gave a small shriek.

In the darkness he must look like a dark huge figure looming over her.

"It's me," he said, and felt anew his shame for deceiving her about who he was.

But even without a name, the sound of his voice seemed to soothe her.

"Oh," she said, "you." And then she reached up and touched the patch over his eye with exquisitely tender fingers. "It's so hard, isn't it? Only seeing with one eye?"

"I think it might be harder than most people imagine."

"I know it is," she said vehemently.

"How would you know that?" he asked, humoring her.

"I tried it. I wanted to know how it felt for you. So I made a patch for my eye. And fell over the coffee table."

For a moment he could barely understand what he had heard, and when it did register, he could barely speak for the lump in his throat, the tightness in his chest.

"You wanted to know what it was like for me?" he repeated, incredulous.

She nodded solemnly, drew his hand to her lips, kissed his fingers. "It's very hard being you," she informed him.

And she didn't know the half of it! But had one other person on the entire face of the earth ever showed such empathy for him?

Had one other person ever cared about him like this? And he was betraying her. He knew who she was, and she didn't have a clue about their shared past. That kind of deception did not a good foundation for a relationship make.

Should he tell her? Or should he back away and not come back?

It occurred to him he was not the only one in over his head. She was in over her head with him.

He needed to stop it.

"Will you come to the wedding reception with me?" she asked groggily. "I wasn't going to go. I changed my mind. I was going to ask you to do something else with me, instead. But I can't remember why. And I so want to see them. Parris and Brad. In love."

That would be as good a place as any to stop it. Right here. Right now. She was talking dreamily about people in love. It was downright scary!

But he found he couldn't refuse her.

She had worn an eyepatch to see what it was like to be him.

And all she wanted was for him to go to a wedding party?

He became aware of feeling he would die for her, if that was asked of him. So, why wouldn't he live for her?

Confusion washed over him. Did he love her? It was turning into a very scary night, and not because she looked even vaguely like Frankenstein's bride. In fact, he wished she did!

"The wedding?" she asked.

The word *no* formed in his mind, firm and hard.

But the word *yes* slipped from his lips. "I'll meet you there."

"Thank you, Bear."

"It's Rick," he said softly.

"Rick," she said. "Oh, I love that name."

"You do?"

"I knew a boy named that once."

Temptation reared its ugly head. How nice it would be to hear how she felt about that boy she had once known.

But it would be one more deception that would be nearly impossible to explain when the time came. If the time came.

"I have to go," he said.

"Please, no," she mumbled, and her hand tightened around his.

He looked down at her again, her hair scattered across the pillow, her eyes closed, her lashes so thick and long they cast small shadows on her cheeks.

She'd had a head injury. You didn't leave people alone who had sustained head injuries. They had to be checked for possible concussion every few hours.

Sighing with resignation, he lay down on top of the covers beside her, being very careful not to make contact.

But she shifted into him, sighed happily and slept.

Cautiously he put his arm around her. Touched her hair, ran his thumb over her cheek and her lips.

It was all wrong. None of this was part of his plan.

So, why did he feel so right? As right as he had felt since his accident? Rick had not slept at night for months, and yet his eyes felt suddenly heavy as the sensation of calm and connection seeped through him. He shut his eyes, telling himself it would only be for a moment…

He awoke to the sound of the adjoining room door rattling. For a moment he felt disoriented, the smell of roses strong around him.

"Cynthia! I'm supposed to check on you every hour."

Her mother!

He turned to her. So, this was what it would be to wake up beside her, to feel such incredible reverence for life, to have a renewed sense that maybe miracles happened to ordinary guys—unworthy guys—just like him.

And then as the rattling on the locked door became more strenuous he kissed her cheek, slipped out of the bed, and out the patio door. The scent of roses seemed to be going with him, and at the last minute, he remembered the rose stuffed into his pocket.

It was wilted and crushed, not much of an offering at all. On the other hand, she was a bit wilted and crushed tonight, too. He laid the fragile rose tenderly on the table on her balcony and slipped into the night.

Before dawn came, he had drawn a roof on his chapel.

Its lines soared upward to that rare place where human beings were allowed to touch the sky, dance with spirit.

Inserted into the lines of the roof, above the center aisle, would be stained-glass panels, so that the bride would walk down that aisle bathed in soft golden light. The glass panel in the ceiling over the altar would be designed so that a dazzling prism of light—indigos and reds and yellows—would dance together and illuminate the bride.

Exhausted, stunned by the beauty of his creation, he set it aside. He had always been a good architect. His work had been called brilliant, and it had won all kinds of professional accolades and awards. He had always felt a tremendous sense of accomplishment when a building he had drawn became a reality. There was something extraordinarily heady about creating something where there had been nothing before.

All those things had helped him erase that sense of not being good enough, had helped him erase a past that had found him wanting. He was a successful architect, not a mechanic's son from the wrong side of the tracks.

But for all that, he would not have ever described himself as inspired. He always missed the mark of what he truly wanted to express by a hair.

His buildings lacked, and now he saw exactly what they had lacked. Heart. Soul.

Technically brilliant, but that mysterious something that separated brilliance from genius had never been his.

And yet, looking at that drawing, he felt awed by it. Suddenly, humbly, he was aware that genius was a gift that poured through a man, that did not belong to him. This inspiration had been given to him because his heart was open in some way that it had not been previously.

Oddly enough, the mechanic's son was very much a part

of the drawing in front of him, his hopes and dreams for a world that contained love were in every line. Oddly enough, his scars were also in the drawing, deepening it, balancing those soaring upward lines.

A month ago, if he had been contemplating open hearts he would have turned it into some kind of cynical joke, maybe about love being comparable to open-heart surgery.

That's what love had been in his home. His mother and father at each other's throats. The unsettled home life had turned Rick Barnett into the quintessential bad boy. The only class he'd ever done well in was shop. He'd loved fast motorcycles, black leather, easy women. His good looks and fun-loving grin had been like a magic key that could open female hearts. When his parents had finally, mercifully, divorced, he had still felt battered. The word *commitment* had not existed in his youthful vocabulary. He had lived by the words of an old rock-and-roll song, made them his motto.

He was here for a good time, not a long time.

And then he had noticed Cynthia Forsythe, a girl every bit as good as he was bad. He'd been intrigued by her. She had no patience for his easy grin. When he teased her and called her Goody Two-shoes she snubbed him so thoroughly he could feel himself disappearing. When he tormented her about her world of rules and regulations, she confirmed he was disappearing by treating him as though he were invisible.

Finally, he had stopped teasing and stopped smiling. He had begged her to give him a chance—one ride on his motorcycle. If she hated it, if she hated him after that, he would let her go. He would never bother her again.

She'd said yes, and his whole world had changed. Because as much as she had been determined to hate his motorcycle and him, she had not. For three glorious weeks, wrapped in the music of her laughter, he had believed in miracles. In love. He had believed his world could be different than it had been. He had hoped.

With Cynthia's arms wrapped around him, her body molded to his as they sat astride a speeding motorcycle, anything in the whole world had seemed possible.

He saw, now, it was inevitable that their different worlds would pull them apart. He had not been able to belong to her world, and she had not been able to defy her mother and come into his. Still, the split had confirmed his suspicion that relationships between men and women could only end in heartache.

And yet here he was, same woman, same scenario. The drawing that had emerged from his hand told it all. He was hoping again. Believing again.

He was in way over his head. What was he going to do?

"Drown or swim," he told himself and then laughed.

All of his life he had followed the path that seemed logical. He had followed the path that made him feel in control, as if he could predict the future, protect himself from unknown variables.

Love would count as an unknown variable!

Love. There was that word, that question, for the second time tonight. Did he love her then?

The answer was quick and resounded through his whole being. The answer was in the drawing he had just produced. The answer was in the hollow feeling of fear in his stomach, and the full feeling of courage in his heart.

He took a deep breath. So, when darkness fell again he would let go of his need to be in control. Tonight he was going to a wedding. And he wasn't going to plot or plan anything, even though that went against his architect's nature.

He was just going to see what happened. And live with the faint hope that it might be good.

Chapter Eight

Cynthia stared at herself in the mirror. Despite the lump on her head, she was a woman transformed.

Less than two weeks ago, she had been a bookish and faintly frumpy assistant to a famous writer who happened to be her mother. Despite the fact that she was twenty-six years old she had always felt like a child, as if she was impersonating an adult and might be discovered at any moment.

But a woman—a one-hundred-percent, full-blooded beautiful woman—looked back at her from the mirror tonight.

She was dressed in a cocktail-length dress, the fabric as gossamer as dragonfly wings. It clung and floated, hinted and showed. The dress was pure feminine magic. It was several different shades, turquoise melting into jade green and back again, and the design of it left one of Cynthia's slender shoulders bare. It hugged the swell of her breast and the smallness of her waist, then fanned out in a dazzling array of color and fabric around her legs. It was part Arabian dancer (shades of *Hot Desert Kisses*?) part Princess Di and part Cynthia Forsythe.

But if the outfit heralded the change in her in outer ways, it was her eyes that confirmed the change was inner, as well

Picking up the colors from the dress, they looked green as jade tonight. They sparkled with life, and hinted at a great capacity to feel deeply. There was a brand-new day dawning in her eyes. She knew it and felt it with deep pleasure.

How was it possible for such a change to happen in such a short time? She had gone from feeling like a wooden puppet to being a living, breathing wondrously alive *person*.

It was like a miracle.

And then it struck her, full-force, exactly what that miracle was. There was only one force in the entire universe that could change a person so miraculously, that could bring the dead to life and the crippled to wholeness.

"Oh my God," she whispered. "I'm in love."

She tried to tell herself it was impossible. It was too soon. She didn't know him well enough. For heaven's sake, she had only just found out his name.

She wasn't even sure if she knew herself well enough! This new, improved version, in particular, made her feel as if she was a bit of a stranger to herself.

But the truth shone back at her out of her eyes.

She knew Bear—Rick, he had told her last night—was no stranger.

Her heart had recognized him from the first moment. And so had her soul. She had been shaken awake from a deep slumber because of him. She was alive, fully and gloriously alive, and she was thrilled and grateful.

She picked up her small matching handbag, did one last check of her makeup. She tried to pull her bangs a little farther down over her bandaged bump on her forehead, but they sprang back to where they wanted to be.

It didn't seem to matter. It didn't put a damper on how she was feeling.

Because Rick had said yes. They were moving forward into a new part of this whole experience. They were going out in public. People would see them together. They would do normal things, eat food and dance.

Could the fantasy stand up to its first reality check?

She felt not a single doubt.

"It's darn near a relationship," she said, hugging herself and doing a happy final twirl in front of the mirror.

The dress floated around the length of her legs. She sighed with satisfaction and headed out the door.

The evening was beautiful, even for a place where beautiful evenings were the norm. A gentle breeze came in off the ocean, and the flowers released the fragrance they had stored during the heat of the day. The moon was a sliver still, but stars shone and blinked. Orion watched over her, and she smiled at him.

Brad and Parris's party was in a large outdoor area that was used for picnics and concerts and family reunions. It overlooked one of the many beaches, and Cynthia had walked by it many times.

But nothing could have prepared her for how it had been transformed tonight.

There were no electrical lights. Instead, the pathway to the area was lit with torches that flickered and leapt against an inky sky, and the entire perimeter of the outdoor area was defined by these torches. Inside them, tables formed a loose ring around a flat wooden dance platform. Each table was covered with a white cloth and contained a vase with an array of white flowers with a candle burning at its center. There were bottles of wine opened and breathing on each table. Candles burned everywhere, little winking lights in the flower beds and tucked among the shrubs. They gave the area a magical feel, as though small, brilliant fairies twinkled everywhere.

Many guests had already arrived. People were milling about, sitting at the tables, and the atmosphere was festive. Chatter and laughter filled the air.

Arbors and temporary walls laced with white flowers and illuminated by torches had been put up to give the sensation that this was a private room, set off from the rest of the world.

Some of the tables were set farther back, and Cynthia found one that was almost in an alcove of shrubs. The flickering light of the torches barely illuminated here, though she could see everything perfectly.

She set her bag on the table to save her seat and then went to congratulate the bride and groom.

Parris was absolutely stunning. Her hair was braided with flowers. Her dress was gorgeous—simple, floor-length white silk with tiny, tiny straps—but she could have been wearing a burlap sack and a buzz cut and she still would have looked like the most beautiful woman in the world. She was radiant.

Brad was one of those handsome self-assured kind of guys that Cynthia could find intimidating. But the look on his face when he gazed at his bride—full of wonder and tenderness—made her see instantly what a good heart he had.

Despite having greeted so many people, Parris seemed thrilled to see her.

"Hey," she said with a naughtiness that did not at all

match the innocence of that dress. "How's the red working out for you? It looks like something is working!"

So, that look Cynthia had seen in her own face in the mirror was visible to others.

"It's a beautiful gathering," Cynthia said evasively. "Thank you for inviting me."

Parris hugged her. "I'm so glad you could come. Now, we wanted things very casual, so there won't be any head table or speeches or anything like that. We've just set up a buffet where people can go help themselves anytime."

There was also a table for gifts, and Cynthia went and put her wrapped parcel on it. She noticed quite a fuss being made over one item that was not wrapped, and she moved closer.

She smiled. A carving was there. Of two dolphins leaping out of the water together, their bond and their joy evident. She would have recognized Rick's work anywhere, and she wondered if the fact that his gift was here meant he was here, too.

Would she recognize him? She had only seen him in the darkest of conditions. She felt so excited that tonight she might glimpse more of him.

She looked around but didn't see anyone who even vaguely resembled him. Not that she thought she would. Just like the bear, you didn't see Rick until he wanted to be seen.

She joined the line at the buffet. She chatted with some people she recognized and then realized Rick might by shy in the bright lights surrounding the buffet table. She filled two plates and went back to her table. Seconds later, she sensed him arrive.

"Hello, Rick," she said, and loved the way his name sounded on her lips.

He bent from behind, kissed her cheek, and then touched his lips to the hollow of her shoulder. He took the seat beside her.

"How are you feeling?" he asked.

"Breathless. Could you kiss my neck again?"

"I meant from the bump on the head," he said wryly.

"Oh! Much better actually. Was I an idiot last night? I'm afraid my memories of it are a little foggy."

"You were charming."

"Is that a polite way of saying I was an idiot?"

"Would it worry you to be an idiot?"

"Yes!"

"You can be whatever you want with me. It won't change how I feel."

She was not sure anyone had ever said anything so nice to her. She slid him a look. His face was swathed in darkness, but even so she could see the dark patch that covered his eye, and some of the scarring that she had not really seen before. She reached up and touched his face, deliberately letting her palm rest on the scar that ran like broken glass from his ear, along his jawbone, down the solid column of his neck. He went very still, tense.

"You can look any way you want with me," she said softly. "It won't change the way I feel."

He snorted cynically. "Be careful what you say, Cynthia."

"I mean it."

"You think you do."

"I think we are about to have our first argument," she said dangerously. "Are you going to tell me how I think? What I feel?"

"That would be presumptuous, wouldn't it?" he said, and the hardness was gone from his tone. "I don't want to fight with you."

He held a large shrimp up to her lips. "Peace?" he suggested.

She took a nip of the shrimp. "All right. We'll postpone this discussion."

"I thought maybe we could not have it at all."

"I knew that's what you thought!"

"Now who is presuming?"

She laughed, and they slipped that easily into a comfort zone. They ate and laughed and talked.

She saw her mother and Jerome come in, and though her mother looked around with avid interest, she did not spot her daughter. Cynthia gave an inward sigh of relief.

"I should have guessed she would be here," Rick said.

Cynthia gave him a startled look. "My mother? You know my mother?"

"No, of course not," he said hastily. "Merry. Merry Montrose."

"Don't you like her?" Cynthia asked, confused by his tone. Merry had just made an arrival on the arm of a very handsome man, very much her junior.

There was wine on each table, and Rick tipped their bottle toward her glass, but she quickly covered it with her hand. She allowed him to change the subject.

"Not tonight." She refused the wine. "I missed most of what we did together last night, and I'm not letting that happen again." Merry slipped from her mind.

"Don't worry, it was nothing too exciting."

"Well, if it had been, I'm sure I wouldn't have forgotten."

"You wanted to show me your pajamas," he said wickedly, "and not the ones with the bunnies on them, either."

"That's not true! But if that's not true, how do you know about the bunnies? Maybe I'll have some of that wine after all. What else did I do? Say?"

"I told you, you were charming."

"And I wanted to believe you, until the pajama thing."

"You didn't want me to leave."

No woman in her right mind would want him to leave, but he wouldn't believe it if she said it, so she didn't.

"So, I lay down beside you," he said softly.

"In my bed?" she squeaked.

"Yes. And I watched you sleep and touched your cheek, your hair."

"Did you?" she whispered.

"You smelled of heaven."

"I did not."

"Mmm-hmm. And you had this little drool coming out of your mouth right here."

He touched the corner of her mouth with his finger. It was enough to make a woman think maybe drool was sexy.

"And after I drooled on you?"

"Then you started snoring."

"Loudly?" she asked, appalled.

"Freight train comin' down the track."

"And you're here tonight? After drool and freight trains. Why?"

"Because you are still you."

Dinner dishes were being cleared away, and a band was coming out. The first strains of music filled the intimate space and Brad and Parris took the dance floor.

They could have been the only ones in the room, so deeply were they lost in each other, so tender was their gaze and their touch.

"Dance?" he asked gruffly, as the first song finished and other couples began to take to the floor.

"Yes." She could have answered nothing else. She took his offered hand and he led her to the floor. The song was slow and romantic. His hand effortlessly found the small of her back and he pulled her to him.

Cynthia felt as if she might have waited her whole life for this moment, to feel so utterly content in another's company, so exhilarated by his smallest touch.

So in love.

Their first dance together faded into another and then another. They stayed toward the edge of the floor, cloaked in darkness, and yet Cynthia felt as though she danced in pure light.

Suddenly a band of light illuminated them, a technical glitch that had to do with the music. Cynthia glanced up in time to see the shattered side of his face in that terrible harsh glare. The damage was worse than she could have prepared herself for.

He stood frozen for a moment, the spotlight on him, and then suddenly he was gone. Cynthia found herself standing alone at the edge of the floor, swaying by herself.

"I knew there was a man!" her mother said.

Cynthia whirled. In those moments of pure magic dancing with him, she had managed to forget her life contained one rather large complication.

Emma Bluebell Forsythe.

Emma looked like a queen tonight in a flowing dark-green Christian Dior gown. She even had her diamond tiara—a relic from her coming-out days—pinned in her newly minted hair.

"There is a man," she said, tapping her foot, her arms crossed over her bosom as if she were a schoolmarm and Cynthia an errant child.

"There was," Cynthia said, scanning the surrounding shrubbery and trees. He was gone so completely it would be easy to believe he was a figment of her imagination.

Except the look on her mother's face clearly said he wasn't.

"He was ugly," her mother said shrilly. "He looked like a monster. No wonder you've been so ashamed of him!"

"Ashamed of him?" Cynthia said, aghast. He was probably near! What if he had heard? "The only one I'm ashamed of right now is you. How could you? How could you judge a person you have never met by their appearance?"

"You know, I've had just about enough of this mother-from-hell attitude!"

"You seem to keep reminding yourself of that title, not me!" Cynthia said. "And you have never earned it more than tonight."

"I don't like the dress, Cynthia. It is way too loud. It gives the wrong kind of message entirely."

"And what message would that be?"

"Ripe," her mother said, cruelly. "Ready."

Cynthia swore under her breath.

"A dress to go with that kind of language."

"You know what? You *are* the mother from hell," Cynthia said in a low angry voice.

"And here comes the man who gave me that title right now," her mother said dangerously as she watched Jerome come across the dance floor toward them. He stopped in front of her mother and his smile faded.

"She does have a man in her life," her mother said tightly. "And she felt no obligation to tell me about that. Can you imagine why, Jerome?"

"Actually, no, I can't."

"I'll tell you why. Because you have planted this notion in her head that I don't have to be shown any respect."

"That's completely untrue," Jerome said, but Cynthia

could have told him to save his breath. She recognized all the signs of a major scene coming on, and her mother was just warming up.

All her life, when her mother had had these moods, Cynthia had done her best to change what her mother was feeling, to avert the coming storm if she could. If the mood was brought on by something Cynthia was doing, she changed it or promised it would never happen again.

A pretty big price to pay to escape someone else's temper and pettiness.

She decided right then and there she was no longer accepting responsibility for her mother's temper.

She caught a glimpse of movement down on the beach.

"Excuse me," she said.

"You are not going anywhere!" her mother said, astounded.

Cynthia didn't even answer, just slid into the shrubs as expertly as Rick had moments ago.

"This is your fault!" she heard her mother say to Jerome.

"It would be very wise of you not to scrap with me, Bluebird."

Something about the quietness of Jerome's tone made Cynthia stop and look back. This sounded as if it was going to be far too interesting to miss.

Jerome was challenging her mother!

"Don't you ever call me that again. In fact, don't ever call me again!"

"Gladly. You're as shrill as a street-corner tart."

Though she thought the remark served her mother right after her own mean-spirited remarks about Cynthia's dress and about Rick, she still felt a thrill of pure terror. No one talked to her mother like that! And her mother momentarily froze, too.

And then she raised her hand and slapped Jerome so hard across his cheek that she turned his head.

He looked slowly back at her, and even from where she stood Cynthia could see the dangerous glitter in his eye.

He reached out, locked Emma's wrist in an iron grip and yanked her to him. He kissed her hard, and she fought against him like a wild cat for all of three seconds.

And then she went very pliant. Unless Cynthia was very much mistaken her mother was kissing him back. Moments later they were making their own way from the party. It looked as if they were heading for Emma's apartment—and in a hurry, too.

Someday, Cynthia decided, she would tell Jerome that, if that kiss was any indication, he was worthy of a role in *Hot Desert Kisses*. Or La Torchere's rendition, *Hot Tropical Kisses*.

She could go get Rick now. It was safe. It looked as if they would be able to dance the night away after all.

Rick was on the beach, kneeling. There was a large pile of sand in front of him, and he appeared to be shaping it. From here they could both see the bear rock.

"That was my mother," she said.

"I gathered."

"I would have introduced you to her, but she's meaner than a rattlesnake."

"I heard."

"Rick, I'm so sorry."

He shrugged. "It's true, isn't it? Ugly. A monster."

"No," she said desperately, trying to come around so she could see his face, but he quickly averted it from her.

"Thank you for coming down here. For not—"

"Stop it," she said. "I didn't come down here because

you're some charity case in need of my pity. I came down here because I love you."

He froze. For a moment she thought he might get up and bolt. But that woman who had emerged from the water the other evening, so sure of what she wanted, so sure of how to get it, grabbed hold of the crisp whiteness of his shirt, dragged him to her with all her strength, and laid her lips on his.

Possessive. Passionate. No pity anywhere in sight.

After a millisecond of hesitation, his lips responded to hers, hot and wanting. Everything faded—the party in the background, the sea in the foreground, the whole world was gone, just like that.

The whole world was his lips claiming hers, the tip of his tongue probing the hollow of her mouth and the ridged edges of her front teeth.

Sensation washed over her, hot and liquid. Her mother had been right. She was ripe; she was ready. And she had never felt anything quite as compelling as this desire.

He pulled away from her, nestled his head in the hollow of her throat and whispered, "You pack more punch than a crate of firecrackers."

"When I'm not drooling and snoring," she agreed.

"Should we go back to the party before something happens that we both regret?"

"I wouldn't regret it," she said softly.

He closed her eyes with his palm, touched the tip of her nose and then gently put her away from him. He refocused on the pile of sand. In moments he had shaped a turret.

"You're building a sand castle," she said, delighted in spite of herself. It wasn't nearly as delightful as being kissed.

"It's what I do. I build things. I'm an architect."

She got down in the sand with him. It was damp and shaped easily under her hands. She shaped a turret of her own. It was lopsided and way fatter on the bottom than the top.

"A turret worthy of a drooling, snoring Frankenstein's bride," she said.

He paused and kissed her on the tip of her nose.

A little more brotherly than she was looking for.

Her shoulder touched his. He did not move away. They worked in companionable silence for a while.

"Last year," he said after a long time, his voice low, "I was working on a big project, a huge office complex. I was walking by a wall that was being put up. There was a machine on the other side of it—a loader. The driver backed up and hit the wall. It toppled like the proverbial pile of bricks."

"On top of you?" she gasped in horror.

"Yes."

"Oh, God, Rick, I am so glad you didn't die."

"Well, if I had died," he pointed out, "you wouldn't have met me, so you wouldn't even know to be glad."

"Quit being so logical," she said, slapping him lightly on the arm. It was a nice arm, too.

"I was buried under quite a pile of concrete and debris. They had to be very careful how they got me out. They had to get all of that stuff off me by hand. It took a long, long time. I lost my eye. My face is badly scarred. My larynx is crushed. I still dream about it at night. I think that's part of why I don't sleep at night anymore. That and the fact that if I go out during the day little kids hide behind their mothers."

"Rick," she said, tortured.

"I'm trying to tell you, Cynthia, that I'm flawed."

"You're telling a woman who drools and snores," she reminded him, trying desperately to let him know it didn't matter to her.

They worked silently, side by side, on the castle.

"You're ruining your dress," he pointed out.

"I like this better than the dress."

"People who loved me before it happened didn't love me after," he said in a low voice.

"I would have loved you after," she said fiercely.

"Cynthia, you can't know that."

"I do."

Suddenly there was a terrible ruckus from the general vicinity of the party. A woman and a man were shouting at each other.

"Something in the air tonight?" Cynthia wondered out loud.

"I grew up with that kind of thing. My parents fought all the time."

"Mine did, too. I think my dad died to escape it."

"So, how does that happen?" he asked. "How does it go from what Brad and Parris had tonight, to that?"

They listened to the shouting.

"I hope you fall off a cliff and die!" the woman screamed hysterically.

"It would be better than spending the rest of my life with you," the man shouted back, underscoring the sad thing Cynthia had just said about her father.

They finished the sand castle, but Cynthia could tell Rick's mood was altered, changed. She could not tease him out of it; she could not bring him back.

She tried desperately. "Rick, I meant it. I'm in love with you."

He went very, very still.

"I need you to trust me," she continued. "I can't go any further like this. I want to know who you are. I want to see you."

"I—I need to think about it."

"All right," she agreed, though she was crushed.

"And if I don't agree?"

"I won't see you again," she said sadly. "I can't. Hiding in the night like this just allows you to keep believing you are less than other people because you are scarred physically. It allows you to be ashamed. I don't want you to be ashamed anymore. And I never, ever plan to be ashamed of you."

"Ah," he said, and his voice was sad, too. "An ultimatum."

Had he not heard any of the rest of it?

"If you must call it that, yes, I suppose it is."

He nodded, got up from the sand castle and brushed the sand off his slacks.

Then he leaned over and kissed her. It was not the passionate kind of kiss they had shared earlier.

She thought she tasted farewell.

"Please," she said. "Meet me right here, in this exact place at noon tomorrow. Meet me in the light, so I can look at you."

He didn't answer.

And then he was gone. After a long time she got up and left, too.

She carefully skirted the party. She had no wish to see either Brad and Parris's happiness, or that other couple who were so far from it.

Two ends of the spectrum. Rick had spoken a tragic truth tonight. That couple fighting had started in the very same place as Brad and Parris, all love and hope.

And so had her parents, once upon a time. And his by the sound of it.

What had happened? What happened in between?

She got up and walked slowly back to her room. She felt ancient, a hundred years old.

* * *

Merry walked onto the beach. Someone had built a sand castle here. She glared at it for a moment and then kicked it down.

The Phipps-Stovers had fought publicly tonight, with no thought at all to the pall they were casting over Brad and Parris's moment.

With no thought at all to what they were doing to her, Merry Montrose, aka Princess Bessart.

They had been her thirteenth couple. What would it mean to the curse if they split up permanently?

"I should have known thirteen was going to be unlucky," she said.

And the evening had started out with such potential! That handsome young pup of a handyman had asked her if she wanted to go to the party with him.

It hadn't been a date, precisely. No, he had just been being kind to an old woman.

Still, how she had enjoyed him and his attention.

And he had seemed not even to notice how old and ugly she was. He seemed to enjoy her as she was.

Which, of course, was totally impossible. Were some people really so bighearted, so generous of spirit, that they didn't make judgments based on looks?

Cynthia looked as if she might be one of those people. By now she must have at least glimpsed the travesty to that young man's face.

Merry had glanced over at her tonight, to see her sitting at that romantic table in the dark with Rick, touching his scarred cheek.

Hope had leapt in her breast. She was within a hair of breaking the curse.

Until the complication of the Phipps-Stovers. After their horrible fight, she had left Alex to come here to the beach, too distressed to be in his company anymore.

"Wait," he had called. "Merry, I have to tell you something. It's important."

But she had waved her hand dismissively at him, and he'd had the good sense not to follow her.

What could possibly be important to her now?

If the Phipps-Stovers were over, it was over. The deadline—her thirtieth birthday—was around the corner. There was no time left, and she had a bad, bad feeling about the longevity of the Phipps-Stovers relationship.

So, it didn't matter if Cynthia and Rick made it or not.

None of it mattered. All her hard work, all her attempts to spread love and goodwill were for nothing. Why, she had almost come to believe in the value of love herself, in the power of it!

In a fit of pure pique she pointed her finger at the rock that sat silently in the sea, like a huge slumbering bear.

"Bear of rock, awake, unlock,
Go and wander earth and sea,
You are of no more use to me."

The rock shimmered in the darkness, wavered and then its outline grew strong, vibrating and luminescent, before it vanished with a loud pop.

Her anger vanished as surely as the rock and she regretted having taken so drastic an action. Perhaps she had been premature, but she was so tired of the whole thing.

She had no more energy for magic, and none whatsoever for romance.

Feeling ancient, as if she was a hundred years old, which apparently she was going to be forever and ever, she walked slowly off the beach and back to the loneliness of her room and her sentence.

Chapter Nine

Rick packed his bags. He was methodical and neat, avoiding the impulse to throw everything in jumbled, zip up, and run. There was no running, anyway. The ferry that left the island ran on its strict once-a-day schedule, without variation. He could not leave La Torchere until tomorrow at 2:00 p.m.

No, methodical suited how hard and cold he felt inside. The frozen emotions were pleasingly familiar, far preferable to the gamut he had run over the past few days.

He had allowed himself to be pulled into a magical place. The drawings he had done of the chapel had reflected his own growing desire to hope and dream and love.

But Emma Forsythe's words rang in his ears. *Ugly. Monster.*

When he was done packing and had set his bags by the door, he went to the table and stared at the finished drawings of the chapel. They did not seem like the drawings of a man who was an ugly monster.

They seemed like the drawings of a man who had glimpsed heaven. And had glimpsed a part of that inside himself, no matter what he looked like outside.

He crumpled the pictures angrily, but found he was not quite ready to throw them away. Throwing them away would not be dramatic enough, anyway. Tomorrow, at exactly the same time that he was supposed to meet Cynthia, he would take them to the clearing and make a ceremony of burning them.

And then he would leave this island and all its temptations far, far behind. He would abandon the feeling that he could rise above what had happened to him. He would indulge no more in the fantasy that his hardship might have made him a better man, more compassionate and more sensitive than he had been before his accident.

He would leave behind, especially, the hope that someone would see what was inside and love that despite what the outside man looked like.

The drawing of the chapel said so clearly what he was inside. That was what he wanted to destroy: the evidence that inside him was a great well of hope and compassion and heart, that inside him was a place that longed for a world made brighter by love.

He snorted. Love. The greatest of truths or the greatest of illusions?

He went to the bathroom, needing busy tasks. A shave. A shower. He regarded himself in the mirror, looked himself full in the face, and found a truth there that was nearly as shattering as the damage he saw.

Rick Barnett suddenly saw it wasn't about his face at all. Not about his blindness, or his scars, or his crushed larynx.

Those things had become a convenient excuse to hide from the very thing that life was all about. He was hiding

from a power that enticed him even as he mistrusted it
heartily.

Love. It always started with great promise. But where
did it go? And how did it go there?

That couple screaming at each other at the party had
reopened a wound that went far deeper than the scars on
his face.

His parents had been so much like that. They seemed
to possess an abiding fury at one another that created a wall
neither of them could break through or climb over or go
around, not even for his sake. The anger had not even sub-
sided with the death of their marriage. In fact, the bitterness had deepened between them, and he had always been
the pawn in the middle.

Before they'd split, his memories of childhood were of
waking up in the night to the sounds of their heated bat-
tles. His days had been booze-scented and filled with his
mother's tears and his father's silences.

His memories were of a child praying hard for love to
win and of a child's fervent and desperate prayers not
being answered.

But was there a time limit on prayers? Was there just
the smallest possibility that his prayer for love was being
answered now?

With Cynthia?

"No," he said out loud, and could feel his fear cloaking
itself in anger.

He had seen pictures of his mother and father's wedding. They had been beautiful. They had looked at each
other with unbridled delight. In every picture they were
linked by a touch—his father's hand on the small of her
back, his mother's hand resting on his shoulder, grazing his
cheek. During the first years the snapshots still contained

smiles, delight, touches, a certain playfulness. His father piggybacking his mother around the backyard, her making an outrageous face at the camera. And then something had changed.

He'd always wondered if that something had been him.

Or maybe it was just the way of the world. There was plenty of evidence that the starry-look-and-kisses stage of a relationship was fleeting, and that misery was forever.

There was proof all around him that the dreams died and left something terrible in their place. It wasn't just his mother and father. It wasn't just that couple tonight. No, it was everywhere. Diana and Charles. J.Lo and Ben. Tom and Nicole.

It didn't last. It couldn't last.

He wished the ferry left right now, right this minute. He showered and shaved but then paced restlessly, until his eyes fell upon the chunk of wood, and the bear called to him.

One last carving, then. One last gift for Cynthia.

Only this one would be real. Not doves and dolphins and water nymphs rising from the water.

No, this one would show life not as he wanted it to be, but life as he knew it to be.

The bear took shape under his knife. It was huge and restless. He carved the danger of this animal into every line and sinew and muscle. The bear was like that capricious thing called love. It could be playful, curious, content, connected, loyal, protective. But that was not the side of the bear Rick wanted to capture or portray. No, he wanted to show the side of the bear that could surface with an amazing lack of warning—savage, formidable, frightening, furious. He wanted to show the side of the bear that could leave an unbelievable swath of destruction in its wake, without half trying.

He would leave it for her, for Cynthia, this latest carving, and when she found it she would understand.

Perhaps she would even be glad that he would not make the rendezvous she had set up for noon.

Was he sorry he was causing her pain? Yes.

But he told himself that he was being gallant in his own way, that a little bit of pain now was preferable to a great deal of pain later.

Rick did not know if Cynthia could love him or not. He did not know, given his family history, if he could love her in the way she deserved to be loved.

He was aware, now, that his outer scars paled in comparison to his inner ones.

It was best to leave the whole thing a fantasy.

The next morning, Cynthia's initial reaction of delight at finding the carving on her patio table died quickly.

She frowned as she studied the brilliant lines and curves. The bear could have breathed it was so real. It was technically as wonderful as the other pieces, but gone was the lightness of spirit.

The bear carving contained a restless energy. It showed perfectly the danger of this animal, the dark side of its power.

She sank down on one of the chairs, holding the wood. She stroked it tentatively. Could love tame such a power?

Cynthia remembered when Merry had first told her the story of the bear who married a woman. She had challenged Cynthia to look at it through her own experience, to see how the story had meaning for her.

Suddenly she was very aware that that exercise could never be accomplished by focusing on the bear, his strengths and his weaknesses.

Rather she would have to look at her own.

The strongest element in the story, stronger even than the love between the bear and the woman, had been the bond between the mother and the daughter.

Cynthia could not help but see the parallel with her own life.

Why had the mother in the legend had so much control over her daughter? Was it cultural? Did she have her daughter's best interests at heart, or her own? Did the bear turn to stone because of the mother's judgments? Or because the daughter was so linked to her mother that the daughter's judgments could only mirror those that had been modeled for her?

Did judgment poison the power of love? Wasn't that what had poisoned her own parents' relationship? Her mother's inability to love and accept unconditionally? Her inability to leash her judgments of her husband, to see his good instead of his bad, to focus on his strengths instead of his weaknesses?

Why didn't the daughter in the tale fight for her husband, even though she had never seen his face? She had felt his hands. She had accepted him in her bed! Why had she let him go? Why hadn't she followed him into the sea?

Suddenly, from the questions came the answer Cynthia sought. She knew what she had to do. Not necessarily for Rick, but for herself.

She got up and knocked on her mother's door.

Her mother, not a morning person, made her knock several times before she opened it, a haughty, unforgiving look on her face.

"We need to talk," Cynthia said, surprised by the gentleness in her own voice.

"Now?" her mother said. "I don't think so. Cynthia, it's too early."

"I need to talk now."

Had she ever put her needs ahead of anyone else's? Certainly never ahead of her mother's.

There was a power in it.

She had lived for obligation and duty. Were they parts of love? Or did genuine love demand more? Personal integrity? The strength to stand up for yourself?

Wouldn't self-love be part, perhaps the biggest part, of the whole love equation? Wouldn't true love say, this is who I am, take it or leave it?

True love would leave no place for masks, for people-pleasing games. She hoped she and her mother would enjoy a relationship like that one day, but it seemed as if they would have to start rebuilding from scratch.

Cynthia sat at the table and ignored her mother showing her annoyance by being rough with the coffee things. Instead Cynthia put her gift, the bear, at the center of the table and studied it.

"That's an ugly piece of art," her mother said grouch ily, finally pouring coffee and sitting down. "It has a certain savagery I find distasteful."

Cynthia supposed that was going to set the tone, but on the other hand, who had put her mother in charge of setting the tone? Who had to accept her attempts to manipulate things?

It was a choice, and feeling a strange delight in her newfound power, Cynthia made it. She came right to the point.

"Mother, you called the man I love ugly last night. You called him a monster."

There was no anger in her tone.

"Well, he was," her mother said defensively. "He looked like a mangy old tomcat who had gotten the bad end of a fight in an alley. And what do you mean, love? You've known him days!"

"I will not allow you to speak of someone I care about like that."

"Allow me?" her mother said, shocked.

"You heard me. Allow you."

"Are you making this man a part of your life, then? I can't bear it."

"That's your choice to make."

"Are you saying you would choose him over me? Over your own mother?"

"Yes," she said, and she heard the strength and conviction in her own voice. A woman was supposed to choose her man over her mother. It was the final rite in growing up. It was a rite of passage.

"He's ugly," her mother said defiantly.

Cynthia got up from the table.

"He's not ugly," Cynthia said quietly. "Nor is this carving of the bear. They both possess enormous strength and power. As do I. The strength and power to decide the course of my own life, to choose for myself whom I will and will not love."

"Cynthia, this is foolishness—"

Cynthia held up her hand. The bear demanded respect. "I won't be helping with your next book, Mom. I'm going to look into opening an art gallery here at La Torchere."

Her mother's mouth worked soundlessly.

"And I'm going to marry the man I love."

"Marry him? Has he asked you?"

Cynthia smiled. "No. I'm going to ask him."

"Cynthia, that is not how things are done!"

"No, Mother, what you mean is that is not how you would do things. I am making my own choices from this moment forward. I am having my own life."

Her mother heard her resolve and saw her daughter's strength.

"I always saw this in you," she said sadly. "A fierce independence. I tried to squelch it. I don't know if that was wrong or right."

"You did it so you could keep me," Cynthia guessed softly. "Not for my good, but for yours."

"I only wanted what was best for you, Cynthia. That is all every mother wants for her child. If you marry a man who is so different from you, it will only bring heartache."

"That's what it brought you, Mother. But it didn't have to. You should have tried embracing his differences instead of constantly trying to mold him into what you wanted him to be. You did the same to me, and now you're going to lose me, too."

"I don't want to lose you," her mother said. "Tell me what I need to do to keep you."

"Let me go with your blessing," Cynthia said.

Her mother looked at her. Cynthia could see the exact moment that Emma saw the truth and the strength and the integrity in her daughter's eyes, because she managed to smile through her tears. "Go then, my beloved daughter," she said. "Go with my blessing."

Cynthia dressed for her noon rendezvous with Rick every bit as carefully as she imagined that Parris had dressed for her special day the night before.

She chose one of her new outfits, raspberry capri pants with a matching tank top. She knotted a white sweater over her bare shoulders. The outfit was sexy and bold, but more than that it made a statement. It was the kind of clothing worn by a woman who knew who she was, who knew her own mind.

At ten to twelve, with her heart in her belly, she made the walk to the beach. It felt as if it took her forever to get there.

The bench she had shared with Merry—only a few days ago, though it felt like a lifetime—was disappointingly empty.

Because he was not here did not mean he was not going to come, she told herself.

But she could feel something in her, an intuition, a fore-boding. She could feel something was wrong. She was un-settled as if a hurricane was brewing though there was not a cloud on the horizon and the air was still.

Her uneasiness increased as she scanned the familiar landscape of the beach. What was wrong?

She couldn't place it. She glanced at her watch. It was noon, exactly.

She looked around, hoping to catch a glimpse of him coming toward her. But the resort seemed deserted, as if she was the only one here.

She looked out to sea, to the familiar bay, trying des-perately to center herself, to hold on to her hope. Her breath caught.

Suddenly she knew what was wrong! The rock was gone from the bay.

Vanished.

"That can't be true," she told herself, as if saying it out loud could change it. She tried to tell herself it was the tide, a trick of shifting waters, but she could see from the wa-terline it was low tide right now, not high. The rock should be at its most visible.

And she knew in her gut, no scientific explanation was going to change what was. She could feel the absence of the rock, as if the sun had blinked out in her universe.

But then, instead of feeling despondent, she felt the great joy of having risked it all for love. With that acceptance, her heart began to beat very fast—the tattoo as primal as the beating of Native drums.

The line between reality and fantasy blurred and then was gone.

Cynthia knew the deeper truth that existed in that place between reality and fantasy. She breathed it. It shimmered along her skin.

The bear was gone from the sea because they were playing out the circle. The bear had come to life again. It had turned from stone to beast in that place where the force of love made all things possible. The bear walked again and waited. For her.

She remembered everything she had read about bears. Every single detail.

But one stood out in her mind.

It said that anyone who had ever walked in a forest had been watched by a bear without having any knowledge that he was there.

She could feel him watching her. She scanned the trees beyond the beach and felt the pounding of her heart slow when she caught the faintest movement on the rock bluff.

He was watching her.

The young woman in the story had been passive. She had let others control her. She had never played a role in the unfolding of her own life.

And in that time that was as it had to be. Her culture and her beliefs had dictated those things—on the same circle, but in a different time.

And with a different woman.

Cynthia rose and crossed the sand toward the trees. With every step, she felt her power growing.

Her power to choose, her ability to be strong.

With every step, she felt herself growing closer to the light.

When she climbed, finally, into the clearing where she had seen movement it appeared to be empty.

She stood very still and then saw something fluttering from the trunk of one of the trees.

A paper was tacked to it. Could this be the movement she had seen from below?

She took down the picture and looked at it. She recognized it as an architect's preliminary sketch.

Her eyes filmed over at the beauty of what she was seeing.

This morning, in the carving of the bear, Rick had shown her what was outside him, the darkness of that outer spirit.

Now, as she took down the picture and studied it closely, she saw what was inside him. Her resolve hardened. She would not let her lover go. She would follow him into the sea, if need be. She would bring him to the place of safety where his wounds could be healed.

"Cynthia."

She turned. He was standing on the edge of the clearing, as if he had always been there, as if he would have walked away if he could have. Tenderly she took in the slouch of his shoulders, the hauntedness of his expression, the way his hands tensed into fists and then untensed.

She saw him, his face, for the first time, in the full light.

And she marveled. For she saw no scars at all.

She saw only his beauty. The unmarked side of his face was gorgeous, his features even and strong, his eye the most intense shade of blue she had ever seen.

No, that wasn't quite correct.

She moved toward him, and her sense of recognizing him deepened, and then, startled, she stopped.

She had seen that exact shade of blue before.

Her mind slowly assembled the information it was receiving.

He was older, of course, and the two very different sides of his face had made it hard to recognize him even in the full light.

"Rick?" she whispered. "Rick Barnett?"

He nodded, sheepish, maybe even ashamed.

She crossed the remaining distance between them, reached out and touched him, both her hands on both sides of his face. She touched his scars and she touched his perfection with equal reverence.

"I was leaving," he confessed, his voice hoarse with held emotion. "I wasn't planning on saying goodbye."

She nodded.

"And I knew who you were. All this time. But I never told you who I was."

She nodded again, her heart unfolding like a flower within her breast.

"Cynthia, I thought I was just flawed outside. But I'm not. I'm just plain old flawed. I don't trust. Can't. I'm hard and cold. I'm—"

She put her fingers to his lips, stopping him.

"You're here," she whispered. That was all that mattered. He had—somehow, someway—overcome all that self-doubt and come to her.

"I don't want to be."

She smiled through her tears. "Sometimes love does for us what we cannot do for ourselves."

He looked hard at her. "Cynthia, I don't think I believe in love. But if I did—" His voice faltered.

"If you did?" she encouraged him softly.

"If I did," he admitted, "it would be you."

"Are you sure you don't want to be here?"

He choked back a groan. "You steal my strength. If I was stronger, I would have gone as soon as I realized you had spotted me up here. As soon as I realized you would come. Cynthia, don't you understand? You deserve better. You deserve a man who is whole in every way."

"So, if you were able to think just of me, you wouldn't be here," she reiterated calmly. "But if you were thinking of yourself, then what?"

"If I was thinking only of myself, I couldn't leave you," he said hoarsely, and then some part of him surrendered and he laid his head in the hollow where her neck joined her shoulder.

Her mother had put her own needs first, always, above her daughter's.

Rick was trying to put Cynthia's needs first, instead of his own.

Only he had a limited understanding of what those needs were.

He had a limited understanding of himself.

"You are not the boy you once were," she said to him softly.

"That's what I'm trying to tell you," he said. "Maybe that's even part of why I didn't want you to see me, to recognize me. Because you might expect me to be what I was before, and I'm not."

"Have you considered the possibility you might be better?" she asked.

"No." He said it harshly and quickly.

"Oh, yes," she said firmly. "I remember that boy. I loved him, too, but not the way I love you. You are deeper and wiser and stronger than that boy was, Rick. And I am deeper and wiser and stronger than that girl was. I am going to marry you," she told him decisively, "and we are going to become deeper and wiser and stronger together, forever."

He pulled back from her.

"Do I have any say in this?" he asked, a trace of a smile beginning to tickle his lips.

"Mmm-hmm. You can say yes."

"No other options?"

"No."

"Cynthia—"

"Just say what your heart wants to say," she told him. "And let me look after my own heart. I know exactly what I need."

"What is your mother going to say about all this?"

"When I was a child, I listened to my mother. In the last few days, I have become the woman I have always wanted to be. And now I listen to my heart."

"Tell me what your heart is telling you," he demanded, one last attempt to chase her away with his harshness.

Solidly, she said, "You are not who you used to be. And I am not who I used to be. The changes in you and in me are not bad. Love is asking us to be more than we were before, Rick. It is lifting us up to that place that is beyond the scars and hurts of this world. We can go to a place of the supernatural, if we accept this challenge."

He studied her for a moment longer, and the smile that had tickled his mouth widened.

And then he threw back his head and laughed.

He let out a whoop of pure joy and celebration, picked her up and whirled her around, danced her around the clearing until they were both breathless from it.

His light and his dark melted together and one did not destroy the other.

Instead, he was made whole.

He waltzed her to the edge of the cliff and called over it, for the whole world to hear, "Rick Barnett loves Cynthia Forsythe. Forever!"

Merry's head lifted at the sound of that joyous masculine voice drifting over La Torchere.

She was out on her very private patio, an ice pack on her head.

He called it again, his declaration of love.

It was so strong, his voice, as if it had never been damaged. She suspected his spirit would be like that, too, made stronger by adversity, not weakened by it.

She wanted to believe in the message that love could make all well with the world.

But could it really?

She stared down at the wrinkles on her hands and knew she faced adversity beyond what she could have ever imagined.

Last night, Alex had been waiting for her outside her room when she got in from her lonely vigil on the beach. He had a touching way of caring about her, an annoying way of ignoring her dismissals, forgetting his place.

Of course, she had soon found out why!

He had given her the shocking news that he was not just a handyman.

He was the owner of the resort!

But what did it matter? Even if she were ever restored to her old self, she was betrothed to another.

And why had he told her his secret? Why had he felt as if it was so important that she know?

He had told her he respected her too much to live a lie in her presence, to spend one more day deceiving her.

Once upon a time, when she was young, she had thought, arrogantly, that she knew everything, and that she had all the answers, for everyone.

But no one had ever respected her. Or at least not for herself. They might have respected her because of her position and her family, out of fear or tradition, but not because of who she was.

But what was that? Who was she? Who had she been then? And who was she now?

Merry felt a dismaying sense of having no answer, and no idea what was right or what was wrong, what was good or what was bad.

What a terrible price she had paid to learn this lesson of humility.

Even with the help of magic, she was not in control of the universe.

Even her own life was out of control. Word had come to her this morning that the Phipps-Stovers had officially separated. Would they divorce?

She had considered interfering, of course, but she had stopped herself. Would she wish them lives of misery, just so that she could go back to being who she once was? Once she would have, unhesitatingly. Now, she wasn't so sure.

His voice came again, beautiful, wild, free, as if his spirit had joined the spirit of his brother, the bear.

"Rick Barnett loves Cynthia Forsythe forever."

All the magic in the world really couldn't make that kind of miracle happen.

Despite herself, she let the strength of Rick's voice wash over her. She felt the power in it.

And despite the fact that it felt weak and foolish to do so, for one shining moment, she allowed herself to believe that maybe, just maybe, there were powers greater than hers looking after the order of things.

Maybe, just maybe, her own story was going to have a happy ending after all.

* * * * *

Don't miss the conclusion of
IN A FAIRY TALE WORLD... Six reluctant couples.
Five classic love stories.
One matchmaking princess.
And time is running out!
TWICE A PRINCESS by Susan Meier
Silhouette Romance #1758 Available March 2005

SILHOUETTE Romance®

presents
a tender love story by reader favorite
Madeline Baker

EVERY INCH A COWBOY
(Silhouette Romance #1760)

Dana Westlake's fragile heart needed time to heal. But with ruggedly handsome ranch hand Chay Lone Elk prowling around, she'd risk everything for a second chance at love.

*Available March 2005
at your favorite retail outlet.*

If you enjoyed what you just read,
then we've got an offer you can't resist!

Take 2 bestselling love stories FREE!

Plus get a FREE surprise gift!

Clip this page and mail it to Silhouette Reader Service™

IN U.S.A.
3010 Walden Ave.
P.O. Box 1867
Buffalo, N.Y. 14240-1867

IN CANADA
P.O. Box 609
Fort Erie, Ontario
L2A 5X3

YES! Please send me 2 free Silhouette Romance® novels and my free surprise gift. After receiving them, if I don't wish to receive anymore, I can return the shipping statement marked cancel. If I don't cancel, I will receive 4 brand-new novels every month, before they're available in stores! In the U.S.A., bill me at the bargain price of $3.57 plus 25¢ shipping and handling per book and applicable sales tax, if any*. In Canada, bill me at the bargain price of $4.05 plus 25¢ shipping and handling per book and applicable taxes**. That's the complete price and a savings of at least 10% off the cover prices—what a great deal! I understand that accepting the 2 free books and gift places me under no obligation ever to buy any books. I can always return a shipment and cancel at any time. Even if I never buy another book from Silhouette, the 2 free books and gift are mine to keep forever.

210 SDN DZ7L
310 SDN DZ7M

Name	(PLEASE PRINT)	
Address	Apt.#	
City	State/Prov.	Zip/Postal Code

Not valid to current Silhouette Romance® subscribers.

Want to try two free books from another series?
Call 1-800-873-8635 or visit www.morefreebooks.com.

* Terms and prices subject to change without notice. Sales tax applicable in N.Y.
** Canadian residents will be charged applicable provincial taxes and GST.
All orders subject to approval. Offer limited to one per household.
® are registered trademarks owned and used by the trademark owner and or its licensee.

SROM04R   ©2004 Harlequin Enterprises Limited

ATHENA FORCE

The Athena Academy adventure continues....

Three secret sisters
Three super talents
One unthinkable legacy...

The ties that bind may be the ties that kill as these extraordinary women race against time to beat the genetic time bomb that is their birthright....

Don't miss the latest three stories in the Athena Force continuity

DECEIVED by Carla Cassidy, January 2005

CONTACT by Evelyn Vaughn, February 2005

PAYBACK by Harper Allen, March 2005

And coming in April–June 2005, the final showdown for Athena Academy's best and brightest!

Available at your favorite retail outlet.